PENGUIN

C000184039

FRANÇOIS

SELECTED POEMS

François Villon was born in Paris in 1431. His real name was de Montcorbier, also called des Loges. He was brought up by his benefactor Guillaume de Villon, chaplain of Saint-Benoît-le-Bétourné, whose name he adopted. He received the degree of Master of Arts in 1452. He killed an ecclesiastic in the cloister of Saint-Benoît in 1455, was pardoned, but later fled from Paris and remained in exile for six years, after taking part in a theft at the College of Navarre. We know that he visited Bourg-la-Reine, Angers, Bourges, Saint-Géneroux, and Blois, where he took part in a poetic contest organized by Charles d'Orléans.

In 1461 Villon was imprisoned by the Bishop of Orléans but was later freed by Louis XI. He was again arrested in 1462 at the Châtelet, on a charge of theft, and, following an affray with a papal notary in 1462, he was condemned to be 'pendu et estranglé' but the sentence was repealed and he was banished from Paris for ten years. He died some time after 1463. His surviving works are *Le Lais* (1456); *Le Testament* (*c.* 1461); *ballades*, which include *Ballade du Concours de Blois*, *Ballade des dames du temps jadis* and the epitaph, *Ballade des pendus*, which he composed when under sentence of death; a few poems and epistles and the *Débat du cuer et du corps de Villon*.

Peter Dale was born in 1938, in Surrey where he still lives. He was educated at Strode's School, Egham, and St Peter's College, Oxford, where he graduated in English in 1963. Currently, with William Cookson, he is co-editor of the literary magazine *Agenda*. In 1976, he published his selected poems, *Mortal Fire*. His sonnet-sequence, *One Another*, appeared in 1978 and his latest book of poems, *Too Much Water*, was published in 1983. His most recent verse-translations are *Narrow Straits*, a selection of nineteenth century French poetry, and *Poems of Jules Laforgue*. He has recently completed a new Book of verse, *Earth Light*.

Selected Poems

François Villon

Chosen and
translated by
Peter Dale

Penguin Books

PENGUIN BOOKS

Published by the Penguin Group
27 Wrights Lane, London W8 5TZ, England
Viking Penguin Inc., 40 West 23rd Street, New York, New York 10010, USA
Penguin Books Australia Ltd, Ringwood, Victoria, Australia
Penguin Books Canada Ltd, 2801 John Street, Markham, Ontario, Canada L3R 1B4
Penguin Books (NZ) Ltd, 182–190 Wairau Road, Auckland 10, New Zealand

Penguin Books Ltd, Registered Offices: Harmondsworth, Middlesex, England

These translations first published in *Villon* by Macmillan 1973
Published in Penguin Books 1978
Reprinted 1988

Copyright © Peter Dale, 1973, 1978
All rights reserved

Printed and bound in Great Britain by
Cox & Wyman Ltd, Reading
Set in Monotype Bembo

Contents

A Note on the Translation 7
A Biographical Note on Villon 10
A Note on the Text 11

Le Lais / The Legacy 12
Le Testament / The Testament 40
Le Debat du Cuer et du Corps de Villon / The Debate between
   Villon's Heart and Body 202
Epistre / Ballade: Epistle 208
Requesté a Monseigneur de Bourbon / Request to Mgr de
   Bourbon 212
Quatrain / Quatrain 216
L'Epitaphe Villon / Villon's Epitaph 218
Louenge a la Court de Parlement / Homage to the Court 222
Question au Clerc du Guichet / Question to the Clerk at the
   Gate 226

Notes 228

A Note on the Translation

'Strict metrical translators still exist. They seem to live in a world untouched by contemporary poetry. Their difficulties are bold and honest, but they are taxidermists, not poets, and their poems are likely to be stuffed birds . . .' So wrote Robert Lowell in his introduction to *Imitations*.

This translation is a strict metrical translation and would seem, from Lowell's remarks, to require justification in modern eyes. It seems to me that to translate a very formal poet into free verse is as odd as to attempt to translate *The Cantos* into heroic couplets. Traffic in either direction is as illogical. The fact is that the exigencies of form that the translator faces are more or less the same as the author faced – and these are part of the texture of the poem. Lowell goes on to recognize this in his introduction: 'A better strategy would seem to be the now fashionable translations into free or irregular verse. Yet this method commonly turns out a sprawl of language, neither faithful nor distinguished, now on stilts, now low, as Dryden would say.' Lowell himself opts for a half-way house: 'I believe that poetic translation – I would call it an imitation – must be expert and inspired, and needs at least as much technique, luck and rightness of hand as an original poem.'

In his practice with Villon, he has fallen between two stools by neither adhering to the strict rhyme-scheme to establish expectancy and rhyme-compulsion nor discarding rhyme altogether:

> Who cares then to die shriven?
> Feet cramp, the nostrils curve,
> eyes stare, the stretched veins hiss
> and ache through joint and nerve –

The gist of this is in the original, except 'nostrils curve' which is clearly rhyme-compulsion and does not add poetry to an otherwise prosaic verse.

My practice has been to use Villon's own ballade stanza as exactly as possible and, like him, to use all the devices of change of tone, exclamation, and seeming irrelevance to master the form. The task is somewhat more difficult in English because of the lack of rhyme-words, not to mention Villon's remarkable skill in rhyming on the exact word, as Pound pointed out.

So much for generalities. It remains true that Villon cannot really be translated; he can only be dislocated. He has muscle and he has music, a mastery of form. In English translation, you cannot convincingly and consistently have all three. I have tried to articulate muscle and bones, the sleight of mood – the music has had to make shift for itself. A ghost of it lingers, I hope, in the more straightforward stanzas.

In a verse translation you cannot always render what a man is saying; you must translate his way of saying. The exigencies of rhyme, idiom, pun and innuendo lead Villon to certain nonchalances of expression and a cavalier attitude to form that cannot always occur at the same point in a language of different idioms and greater problems in rhyme. For example, in the middle section of *Le Lais*, with its knockabout humour, I have used the occasional Hudibrastic rhyme which clearly conveys the mood in English though there is no equivalent in French with its different rhyme-system.

Villon's subject has further created more localized problems. The will-form requires that phrases like 'I give'; 'I bequeath'; 'I leave' regularly open stanzas. They are awkward rhyme words in English so a degree of inversion is required. (The original is not without inversion.) This problem is deepened by the fact that things are left to proper names, which, being French, have to be kept from the end of the line or anglicized.

So much for the letter; it is the spirit one needs to translate. Apart from the formal challenge, what interested me was Villon's voice, the paradoxical moods he controls: the nonchalant concern; the sad gaiety; the gallows humour; the arrogant humility (and vice versa); the comic pathos – the energy, verve and the sheer music.

No version of Villon can satisfy for long. If this one opens again the possibility of strict metrical translation it will have lasted long enough.

If it does, William Cookson, who encouraged me in the project and supplied many texts I have used, must take chief credit. I am equally indebted to the versions of Anthony Bonner of *Complete Works of François Villon* (Museum Press, London, 1960) and to Galway Kinnell's versions in *The Poems of François Villon* (Signet Classics, 1965). Swinburne's, Lowell's, Wilbur's, and, most of all, Tom Scott's versions have been of great assistance in deciding what one may or may not get away with in a verse translation. I am also very grateful to Mr Stanley Burnshaw whose criticism of the translation has led to improvements in the versions in this bilingual edition.

PETER DALE

A Biographical Note on Villon

François Villon was born François Montcorbier or François des Loges in Paris in 1431. He took his surname, Villon, from his guardian and benefactor, Guillaume de Villon, chaplain of Saint-Benoît-le-Bétourné, a man of whom he speaks well in both *Le Lais* and *Le Testament*. He took his *baccalauréat* from the University of Paris in 1449. Around 1451, he was probably involved in a student rag which removed a landmark (le Pet au Diable: The Devil's Fart) from the front of Mademoiselle de Bruyère's house. He himself mentions a poem, *Le Roman du Pet au Deable*, in *Le Testament*. However, in 1452, he received his *licence* and *maître ès arts* from the University of Paris. His first clash with the law occurred in 1455 when he was involved in a fight with a priest who was killed. An eye-witness, admittedly a friend of Villon's, maintains that he acted in self-defence. Though pardoned for the murder in 1456, that same year he was implicated in the famous robbery of five hundred golden *écus* from the College of Navarre. Guy Tabary and Colin de Cayeux are two of his confederates mentioned in *Le Testament*. In this year he wrote, presumably in some haste, *Le Lais*. Tabary's confession to the robbery in 1457 made Villon leave Paris and go on the run. Much of the rest of the detail of his life comes from *Le Testament*, on the assumption that it is truly autobiographical. According to this he was imprisoned, somewhat unjustly or pettily if his mood is anything to judge from, by the Bishop of Orleans in his palace-dungeons at Meung. He was set free to celebrate King Louis XI's progress through the town. In this year he wrote *Le Testament* in which he speaks of wanderings and various towns that must have been his itinerary between, say, 1456 and 1461. In 1462, he is again in prison, the Châtelet, charged with the robbery of the College of Navarre. He was released quickly on promising to repay the money. The last real fact we have about Villon is his arrest for brawling later in 1462. Although he seems to have been a mere onlooker he was sentenced to death. Parliament set aside the sentence, imposing banishment from Paris.

A Note on the Text

This text has been prepared to follow the sense accepted from various sources in the course of translating. I am no scholar of medieval French; the variants and pointing I have accepted have no greater support than that I thought at the time they yielded the best poetry. I have pointed out some of the main deviations from the usual text in footnotes.

P.D.

Le Lais

I

L'an quatre cens cinquante six
Je Françoys Villon escollier
Considerant, de sens rassis,
Le frain aux dens, franc au collier,
Qu'on doit ses œuvres conseillier
Comme Vegece le raconte,
Sage Rommain, grant conseillier,
Ou autrement on se mesconte ...

2

En ce temps que j'ay dit devant
Sur le Noel, morte saison,
Que les loups se vivent de vent
Et qu'on se tient en sa maison
Pour le frimas, pres du tison,
Me vint ung vouloir de brisier
La tres amoureuse prison
Qui souloit mon cuer debrisier.

3

Je le feis en telle façon,
Voyant celle devant mes yeulx
Consentant a ma desfaçon,
Sans ce que ja luy en fust mieulx –
Dont je me dueil et plains aux cieulx
En requerant d'elle venjance
A tous les dieux venerieux
Et du grief d'amours allejance.

The Legacy

1

Fourteen fifty-six was the year
when I, François Villon by name,
a scholar, mind and senses clear,
champing the bit and feeling game,
knowing that one must judge one's fame
and works as Vegetius truly states,
wise Roman, counsellor without blame,
or otherwise one miscalculates . . .[1]

2

At this time as I said before,
at Christmas-tide, the dead season,
when wolves live off the winds that roar
and people stay indoors with reason,
beside the fire now there's a freeze on,[2]
there came to me an urge to shake
off all the chains of love – though treason –
that seize my heart till it would break.

3

And so I did it in this way,
seeing her always before me go,
permitting my destruction, day
by day, no happier for it though.
I grieve to heaven that this is so,
and pray for vengeance from the gods
of love, and plead again they show
mercy on those that love at odds.

4

Et se j'ay prins en ma faveur
Ces doulx regars et beaux semblans
De tres decevante saveur
Me trespersans jusques aux flans
Biens ilz ont vers moy les piez blans
Et me faillent au grant besoing.
Planter me fault autres complans
Et frapper en ung autre coing!

5

Le regart de celle m'a prins
Qui m'a esté felonne et dure.
Sans ce qu'en riens aye mesprins,
Veult et ordonne que j'endure
La mort, et que plus je ne dure.
Si n'y voy secours que fouïr.
Rompre veult la vive souldure
Sans mes piteux regretz oïr.

6

Pour obvier a ces dangiers
Mon mieulx est, ce croy, de partir.
Adieu, je m'en vois a Angiers,
Puis qu'el ne me veult impartir
Sa grace, ne la me departir.*
Par elle meurs, les membres sains,
Au fort, je suis amant martir
Du nombre des amoureux sains.

*The Longnon-Foulet text reads: 'Sa grace, il me convient partir.'
Anthony Bonner reads: 'Sa grace, ne me departir' (*The Complete Works of
François Villon*, Museum Press, London, 1960). The Longnon-Foulet also
reads, in line 2, 'fouïr' for 'partir'. I prefer the richer rhyme. I have
followed Kinnell's version in *The Poems of François Villon*, Signet Classics,
New York, 1965.

4

I took it all as in my favour:
fine appearances, soft glance,
but double-crossing her behaviour,
she tortured me on my own lance.
She savaged me, and not by chance
she showed so clean a pair of heels.
In my great need she would not answer:
I must go plough in other fields.[3]

5

The eyes of her had taken me,
she who had double-crossed me so.
I'd done no harm that I could see
and yet her wish commands I go
to death and be no more. I know
there's little I can do but leave.
She'd cut me dead with a single blow
and never hear my last words heave.

6

It would, I think, be wise to go
and dodge these dangers now. Good-bye,
I'm off to Angers. She gives me no
favour, not a bit.[4] I die
in her though sound in health. Yet I,
the martyred lover, rise above
all this and I'll be counted high
numbered among the Saints of Love.

7

Combien que le depart me soit
Dur, si faut il que je l'eslongne.
Comme mon povre sens conçoit
Autre que moy est en quelongne,
Dont oncques soret de Boulongne
Ne fut plus alteré d'umeur.
C'est pour moy piteuse besongne.
Dieu en vueille oïr ma clameur !

8

Et puis que departir me fault
Et du retour ne suis certain –
Je ne suis homme sans desfault
Ne qu'autre d'acier ne d'estain –
Vivre aux humains est incertain
Et après mort n'y a relaiz,
Je m'en vois en pays loingtain;
Si establis ce present laiz.

9

Premierement, ou nom du Pere,
Du Filz et du Saint Esperit
Et de sa glorieuse Mere
Par qui grace riens ne perit,
Je laisse, de par Dieu, mon bruit
A maistre Guillaume Villon,
Qui en l'onneur de son nom bruit –
Mes tentes et mon pavillon.

7

However hard it comes, I must
now leave her to it. My dim wit
conceives that someone else has thrust
his shuttle in and out a bit.
No Boulogne kipper on the spit
dried out of humour more than me.
A sorry business, all of it.
– Pray God may hear my misery.

8

And since I now must leave my place
and lack assurance of return
(I'm not a man without a trace
of blame, nor made of stuff more stern
than most, no iron or steel concern),
since human life's uncertain still
and death no rescue, since I yearn
for a far country, I make my will.

9

First, in the Name of Father, Son,
the Holy Ghost and Our Lady's Grace
that leaves no soul for lost, not one,
I leave (D.V.) in pride of place
my fame that rumour yet may trace
back to the honour of his name,
to Guillaume Villon – in any case,
my tents and pavilion to the same.

10

Item: a celle que j'ai dit,
Qui si durement m'a chassié
Que je suis de joye interdit
Et de tout plaisir dechassié,
Je laisse mon cuer enchassié:
Palle, piteux, mort et transy.
Elle m'a ce mal pourchassié
Mais Dieu luy en face mercy.

11

Item: a maistre Ythier Marchant
Auquel je me sens tres tenu,
Laisse mon branc d'acier tranchant –
Ou a maistre Jehan le Cornu –
Qui est en gaige detenu
Pour ung escot huit solz montant.
Si vueil selon le contenu
Qu'on leur livre, en le rachetant.

12

Item: je laisse a Saint Amant
Le Cheval Blanc, avec *la Mulle*;
Et a Blarru mon dyamant
Et l'*Asne Royé* qui reculle;
Et le decret qui articulle
Omnis utriusque sexus
Contre la Carmeliste bulle,
Laisse aux curez, pour mettre sus.

10

Item: to the lady mentioned above
who overturned my applecart
and drove me from the joys of love,
I leave the relic of my heart,
pale, piteous and dead. Her part[5]
it was that tossed me to this fate
and ruined pleasure for a start:
may God show mercy on her state.

11

Item: To Ythier Marchant[6] – I feel
obliged to him somehow – or was it
Jean le Cornu? I leave my steel
sword, razor sharp. But no deposit
as it's in pawn. And not to cosset
either of them, I hereby pray
it's given both – only because it's
what they'll ask for if they pay.

12

Item: to St Amant,[7] *The White Horse*
to make a pair with *The She-Mule*;
and to Blarru[8] I give, of course,
my diamond, that costly jewel,
or bucking *Zebra*. I leave the rule
Omnis utriusque sexus . . .[9] (fence
for the Carmelite bull) to clerics who'll
be stuck enforcing so much sense.

13

Et a maistre Robert Valee,
Povre clerjot en Parlement,
Qui n'entent ne mont ne vallee,
J'ordonne principalement
Qu'on luy baille legierement
Mes brayes estans aux *Trumillieres*
Pour coeffer plus honnestement
S'amye Jehanne de Millieres.

14

Pour ce qu'il est de lieu honneste
Fault qu'il soit mieulx recompensé
Car le Saint Esperit l'admoneste
Obstant ce qu'il est insensé.
Pour ce, je me suis pourpensé
Puis qu'il n'a sens ne qu'une aulmoire
(A recouvrer sur Maupensé)
Qu'on lui baille *l'Art de Memoire*.

15

Item: pour assigner la vie
Du dessusdit maistre Robert –
Pour Dieu, n'y ayez point d'envie ! –
Mes parens, vendez mon haubert
Et que l'argent, ou la plus part,
Soit emploié dedans ces Pasques
A acheter a ce poupart
Une fenestre emprès Saint Jaques.

13

But first and foremost I command
that master Rob Vallée [10] (a poor
clerk to the parliament who can't
tell hip from whore) receive before
I go my trousers for his whore,
Jeanne de Millières. Though now in hock
down in *The Greaves*, they'll look the more
her style than any kind of frock.

14

And since his family's well heeled
he must receive more recompense
(The Holy Ghost would have me yield)
because it's clear he's somewhat dense.
It seems to me to make good sense
to give – as cupboards have more brains –
(should Tom Fool manage to dispense
with it) *The Art of Memory*'s remains.

15

Item: that master Rob may make
himself some sort of livelihood
(and don't be jealous for Christ's sake)
my parents are to get a good
price for my coat of mail and should,
with part, before it's Easter, buy
that mutt a stall and have it stood
beside St Jacques and let him try.

16

Item: laisse et donne en pur don
Mes gans et ma hucque de soye
A mon amy Jacques Cardon,
Le glan aussi d'une saulsoye,
Et tous les jours une grasse oye,
Et ung chappon de haulte gresse;
Dix muys de vin blanc comme croye,
Et deux procès, que trop n'engresse.

17

Item: je laisse a ce noble homme
Regnier de Montigny, trois chiens;
Aussi, a Jehan Raguier, la somme
De cent frans prins sur tous mes biens.
Mais quoy? Je n'y comprens en riens
Ce que je pourray acquerir.
On ne doit trop prendre des siens,
Ne son amy trop surquerir.

18

Item: au seigneur de Grigny
Laisse la garde de Nijon
Et six chiens plus qu'a Montigny,
Vicestre, chastel et donjon.
Et a ce malostru chanjon,
Mouton, qui le tient en procès,
Laisse trois coups d'ung escourjon
Et couchier paix et aise es ceps.

16

Item: to Jacques Cardon,[11] my friend,
in outright gift I leave my cape
and gloves, and further, at my end,
some willow seed of acorn shape
and every day without escape:
a fleshy goose and capon fat;
ten hogsheads more of chalk than grape;
two briefs. He won't gain much on that!

17

Item: I leave that noble man
de Montigny,[12] three hounds of mine;
Jean Raguier, all that I can:
a hundred francs I will assign
from all my rents – but draw the line
at any increase with the rents.
Kin shouldn't always buy the wine,
nor friends make up your lost percents.

18

Item: to Grigny's Lord[13] I give
the watch-tower of Nijon, add
Bicêtre dungeons in which to live,
and six more dogs than Montigny had.
For Mouton, the bastard, nothing's too bad:
three lashes for taking him to court,
and after that he might be glad
to sleep at ease in chains too short.

19

Et a maistre Jaques Raguier
Laisse l'Abruvouër Popin;
Pesches, poires seur gras figuier;★
Tous jours le chois d'ung bon loppin;
Le trou de *la Pomme de Pin*,
Clos et couvert, au feu la plante,
Emmailloté en jacoppin,
Et qui voudra planter si plante!

20

Item: a maistre Jehan Mautaint
Et maistre Pierre Basanier,
Le gré du seigneur qui attaint
Troubles, forfaiz, sans espargnier.
Et a mon procureur Fournier,
Bonnetz cours, chausses semelees,
Taillees sur mon cordouannier
Pour porter durant ces gelees.

21

Item: a Jehan Trouvé bouchier
Laisse *le Mouton* franc et tendre
Et ung tacon pour esmouchier
Le Beuf Couronné qu'on veult vendre
Et *la Vache* – qui pourra prendre
Le vilain qui la trousse au col.
S'il ne la rent, qu'on le puist pendre
Et estrangler d'ung bon licol!

★Longnon–Foulet reads 'Pesches, poires, sucre, figuier'.

19

To Master Raguier,[14] I leave
the Popin Trough, a peach and pear
from the tree of figs. May he receive
the standing choice of titbits there;
that hole *The Pine Cone Inn*, his lair,
where cloaked up like a Jacobin,
secret and close, he'll have his share
and those who plough can get stuck in.

20

Item: to Jean Mautaint,[15] I give –
to Pierre Basanier, a life share –
their lord's goodwill, so punitive
in prosecuting crime. To wear
during these days of icy air,
I leave my lawyer[16] the leather tights
and caps my cobbler with such flair
tailored according to his lights.

21

Item: Jean Trouvé,[17] butcher, I leave
The Sheep, so fat and fresh and male;
a cat o' nine tails, he'll receive;
The Horny Ox that's still for sale
and let him knock flies off her tail;
The Cow, if someone gets the bloke
knocking her off on his back. Fail,
and in her harness may he choke.

22

Item: au Chevalier du Guet
Le Hëaulme luy establis;
Et aux pietons qui vont d'aguet
Tastonnant par ces establis
Je leur laisse ung beaux riblis,*
La Lanterne a la Pierre au Let.
Voire, mais j'auray *les Troys Lis*
S'ilz me mainent en Chastellet!

23

Item: a Perrenet Marchant,
Qu'on dit le Bastart de la Barre,
Pour ce qu'il est tres bon marchant
Luy laisse trois gluyons de fuerre
Pour estendre dessus la terre
A faire l'amoureux mestier.
Ou il luy fauldra sa vie querre
Car il ne scet autre mestier.

24

Item: au Loup et a Cholet
Je laisse a la fois ung canart
Prins sur les murs comme on souloit
Envers les fossez, sur le tart;
Et a chascun ung grant tabart
De cordelier jusques aux piez;
Busche, charbon et poix au lart,
Et mes houseaulx sans avantpiez.

---

*Longnon-Foulet reads 'Je leur laisse deux beaux riblis'. I follow other
sources here merely for ease of translation.

22

Item: the Captain of the Watch[18]
I give *The Helmet*. To his men
on foot and groping leg and crotch
along the stalls, I leave them then
a lively larceny, that den
The Lantern in the Stone-milk Lane.
The Lily Pad is mine, though, when
they run me into jail again.

23

To Perrenet,[19] who's widely called
the Bastard of the Bar, I give
three bales of straw to be installed
upon his boards that make one stiff
because his trade's so calmative
and lovingly done. Or he must beg.
He knows no other way to live
and both require a nifty leg.

24

Item: to Wolf and Cholet,[20] I wish
to leave a duck poached from the walls
the way we always catch the dish
inside the moat when darkness falls;
to both I grant to hide their hauls
a monkish cloak down to the feet.
My capless boots I give them also,
kindling, charcoal, peas and meat.

25

Item: je laisse en pitié★
A trois petis enfans tous nus
(Nommez en ce present traictié)
Povres orphelins impourveus,
Tous deschaussiez, tous desvestus
Et desnuez comme le ver –
J'ordonne qu'ilz soient pourveus,
Au moins pour passer cest yver:

26

Premierement, Colin Laurens,
Girart Gossouyn et Jehan Marçeau
– Despourveus de biens, de parens,
Qui n'ont vaillent l'ance d'ung seau:
Chascun de mes biens ung fesseau,
Ou quatre blans, s'ilz l'ayment mieulx.
Ilz mengeront maint bon morceau,
Les enfans, quant je seray vieulx.

27

Item: ma nominacion
Que j'ay de l'Université
Laisse par resignacion
Pour seclurre d'aversité
Povres clers de ceste cité
Soubz cest *intendit* contenus.
Charité m'y a incité,
Et Nature, les voiant nus.

★Longnon-Foulet and Bonner open this stanza with 'De rechief...'
instead of the usual 'Item...'

25

Item: and now for pity's sake,
and three small kids all naked there,[21]
(cited below) I hereby make
provision. Orphans in need of care,
shoeless they are, and going bare
as worms. I leave enough to raise
at least a clout or two to spare
and last them through the darkest days.

26

First, Colin, Girard next, and John,
Goussin, Laurens, Marceau, by birth;
they have no goods, their guardians are gone.
They couldn't raise a bucket's worth.
I parcel them my lands on earth,
or four bob each if they want pay.
Delicate tasters shall cram their girth –
and long before I'm old and grey!

27

Item: my letters of nomination
had from the University
I leave now by my resignation
to shelter from adversity
poor clerks whose names and quality
I list below. Done, I confess,
in good will and humanity,
seeing them in their nakedness.

28

C'est maistre Guillaume Cotin
Et maistre Thibault de Victry,
Deux povres clers parlans latin,
Paisibles enfans, sans estry,
Humbles, bien chantans au lectry.
Je leur laisse cens recevoir
Sur la maison Guillot Gueuldry
En attendant de mieulx avoir.

29

Item: et j'adjoings a la crosse
Celle de la rue Saint Anthoine
Ou ung billart de quoy on crosse,
Et tous les jours plain pot de Saine.
Aux pijons qui sont en l'essoine
Enserrez soubz trappe volliere,
Mon mirouër bel et ydoine
Et la grace de la geolliere.

30

Item: je laisse aux hospitaux
Mes chassiz tissus d'arigniee;
Et aux gisans soubz les estaux,
Chascun sur l'œil une grongniee,
Trembler a chiere renfrongniee,
Megres, velus et morfondus,
Chausses courtes, robe rongniee,
Gelez, murdris et enfondus.

28

Master Guillaume Cotin, and one
Thibaud de Vitry, a pair of poor
latinate clerks of whom there's none
less quarrelsome, nor any more
peaceable – singers who adore
to sing in choir – I leave arrears
of rent on Gueldry's to restore
their wealth till something else appears.

29

I add to their croziers the crook
from Rue St Antoine, or billiard cues
to cross themselves when off the hook,
and Seine in mugs each day to booze.[22]
I give all those with nothing to lose,
the jailbirds clipped and caged for life,
my mirror's fine, untarnished views
and favours from the jailor's wife.

30

Item: I leave to hospitals
my cobweb-leaded window panes.[23]
To people lying under stalls,
a black eye each for them remains,
and may they tremble, face all pains,
shivering, unshaven, starved and thin,
frozen and bashed about the brains,
in tatty clothes that soak the skin.

31

Item: je laisse a mon barbier
Les rongneures de mes cheveulx
Plainement et sans destourbier;
Au savetier mes souliers vieulx;
Et au freppier mes habitz tieulx
Que – quant du tout je les delaisse –
Pour moins qu'ilz ne cousterent neufz
Charitablement je leur laisse.

32

Item: je laisse aux Mendians,
Aux Filles Dieu et aux Beguines
Savoureux morceaulx et frians,
Flaons, chappons, grasse gelines;
Et puis preschier les Quinze Signes,
Et abatre pain a deux mains.
Carmes chevauchent noz voisines
– Mais cela, ce n'est que du mains.

33

Item: laisse *le Mortier d'Or*
A Jehan, l'espicier de la Garde,
Une potence de Saint Mor
Pour faire ung broyer a moustarde.
– A celluy qui fist l'avant garde
Pour faire sur moy griefz exploiz,
De par moy saint Anthoine l'arde !
Je ne luy feray autre laiz.

31

Item: the clippings of my hair,
in full and outright gift, I leave
my barber; and the clothes I wear
the rag-and-bonemen may receive
in the same condition as I leave
them off. My snob I give each shoe
when soleless – my charity achieve
for less than what they cost me new.

32

Item: I bequeath to wandering Friars,
Beguines, and all the Daughters of God,
dainty titbits (that always inspires)
plump hen, capon, piece of cod,
and custard pies. And then, how odd,
to preach the Fifteen Signs and grub
their bread. What's more, the Carmelite squad
mount on our wives. That's the least rub.

33

I leave to John the Guard,[24] who deals
in spice, a crutch and *The Golden Mortar*
to help him stand when least he feels
like mixing mustard with his water.
And that bastard who gave no quarter
and wore the hairs out of my head,
St Anthony take him by the shorter.
That's all he'll get when I am dead.

34

Item: je laisse a Merebeuf
Et a Nicolas de Louvieux
A chascun l'escaille d'ung œuf
Plaine de frans et d'escus vieulx!
Quant au concierge de Gouvieulx,
Pierre de Rousseville, ordonne
Pour le donner entendre mieulx
Escus telz que le Prince donne.

35

Finablement, en escripvant
Ce soir, seulet, estant en bonne,
Dictant ce laiz et descripvant,
J'oïs la cloche de Serbonne
Qui tousjours a neuf heures sonne
Le Salut que l'Ange predit;
Si suspendis et mis en bonne*
Pour prier comme le cuer dit.

36

Ce faisant, je m'entroublié –
Non pas par force de vin boire,
Mon esperit comme lié;
Lors je sentis dame Memoire
Reprendre et mettre en son aumoire
Ses especes collateralles;
Oppinative, faulce et voire;
Et autres intellectualles;

*Longnon-Foulet reads 'Si suspendis et y mis bonne'.

34

Item: to Merbeuf[25] I bequeath,
and Nick de Louvieux – one each,
an eggshell filled with francs beneath
and crowns on top. And just to teach
a lesson well within his reach,
to Pierre de Rousseville I leave
the paper money, free as speech,
his Prince hands out and fools receive.

35

And last, while writing this tonight,
in pleasant mood arranging rhyme
and listing all the items right,
I heard the bell of Sorbonne chime.[26]
It always rings that sound at nine:
the Promise of Salvation made.
And so I lingered on this line
and as my heart desired, I prayed.

36

With this, I must have started dozing
(and not from any wine I'd drunk.)
My mind was half entranced, supposing
I saw Dame Memory open her trunk
and stack on shelves this ancient junk:
dependent species; then came some
opinative; some true, some bunk,
some intellectual, but mostly dumb.[27]

37

Et mesmement l'estimative,
Par quoy prospective nous vient;
Similative; formative,
Desquelles souvent il advient
Que par leur trouble homme devient
Fol et lunatique par mois.
Je l'ay leu – se bien m'en souvient –
En Aristote aucunes fois.

38

Dont le sensitif s'esveilla
Et esvertua fantasie
Qui tous organes resveilla
Et tint la souvraine partie
En suspens et comme amortie
Par oppression d'oubliance
Qui en moy s'estoit espartie
Pour monstrer des sens l'aliance.

39

Puis que mon sens fut a repos
Et l'entendement demeslé,
Je cuidé finer mon propos.
Mais mon ancre trouvé gelé
Et mon cierge trouvé soufflé;
De feu je n'eusse peu finer;
Si m'endormis, tout enmouflé,
Et ne peus autrement finer.

37

She added those estimative
(by which we prophesy events)
conceptual ones and formative
by which, they say, to all intents
a troubled man might lose his sense
and go insane by the moon's light.
– It's Aristotle, this immense
learning, if memory serve me right.

38

But then Sensation pulled a wire[28]
and this incited Fantasy
to stir my organs and the higher,
the sovereign part of you and me,
in rigor mortis seemed to be,
oppressed by my forgetfulness –
which then dispersed and came quite free
to prove itself a sense no less.

39

After my mind had come to rest
my wits began to clear again.
I tried to end the work as best
I could. My ink was frozen then,
the candle blown out God knows when,
and since there was no other light
by which to finish with the pen,
with mittens on, I slept all night.

40

– Fait au temps de ladite date
Par le bien renommé Villon,
Qui ne menjue figue ne date,
Sec et noir comme escouvillon.
Il n'a tente ne pavillon
Qu'il n'ait laissié a ses amis,
Et n'a mais qu'ung peu de billon
Qui sera tantost a fin mis !

Signed, sealed and settled on the date
mentioned above by well renowned
Villon who shits no figs or dates,[29]
and like a mop is caked and browned.
Tents and pavilion, while of sound
body and mind, he leaves to friends.
He has in change less than a pound
and that won't last, the way he spends.

Le Testament

1

En l'an de mon trentiesme aage,
Que toutes mes hontes j'eus beues,
Ne du tout fol, ne du tout sage,
Non obstant maintes peines eues
Lesquelles j'ay toutes receues
Soubz la main Thibault d'Aussigny –
S'evesque il est, seignant les rues,
Qu'il soit le mien je le regny.

2

Mon seigneur n'est, ne mon evesque,
Soubz luy ne tiens, s'il n'est en friche.
Foy ne luy doy n'hommage avecque.
Je ne suis son serf ne sa biche.
Peu m'a d'une petite miche
Et de froide eaue tout ung esté.
Large ou estroit, moult me fut chiche.
Tel luy soit Dieu qu'il m'a esté !

3

Et s'aucun me vouloit reprendre
Et dire que je le mauldis
Non fais – se bien le scet comprendre.
En riens de luy je ne mesdis.
Vecy tout le mal que j'en dis:
S'il m'a esté misericors
Jhesus, le roy de Paradis,
Tel luy soit a l'ame et au corps !

The Testament

1

In the thirtieth year of my age
when I had swallowed up my shame,
not wholly foolish, nor yet a sage,
despite the harm and all that came
from Thibault d'Aussigny[1] by name.
Bishop he may be, blessing streets,
but I repudiate the claim
that he is mine, for all his feats.

2

He's neither lord nor bishop to me.
I had nothing from him but sheer
waste, and return no loyalty.
I'm not his serf or little deer.[2]
He fattened me for half a year
on one small loaf and water free.
Generous? Tight? A sow's ear.
God deal with him as he with me.

3

If anyone must needs complain
and say I damn the man – not so,
if you can see what I maintain.
I deal in no detraction, though.
Here's all the ill of him I know:
if once he's shown me his compassion,
may Christ, the King of Heaven, show
mercy on him in equal fashion.

4

Et s'esté m'a dur et cruel
Trop plus que cy ne le raconte,
Je vueil que le Dieu eternel
Luy soit donc semblable a ce compte.
Et l'Eglise nous dit et compte
Que prions pour noz ennemis?
Je vous diray: 'J'ay tort et honte,
Quoi qu'il m'ait fait, a Dieu remis.'

5

Si prieray pour lui de bon cuer –
Et pour l'ame de feu Cotart!
Mais quoy? ce sera donc par cuer,
Car de lire je suis fetart.
Priere en feray de Picart.
S'il ne la scet, voise l'aprendre,
S'il m'en croit, ains qu'il soit plus tart,
A Douai ou a l'Isle en Flandre.

6

Combien, se oÿr veult qu'on prie
Pour luy, foy que doy mon baptesme –
Obstant qu'a chascun ne le crye –
Il ne fauldra pas a son esme!
Ou Psaultier prens, quant suis a mesme,
Qui n'est de beuf ne cordouen,
Le verselet escript septiesme
Du psëaulme *Deus Laudem* . . .

4

Yet if he were so hard on me,
far worse than I can ever tell,
I ask the Lord of Eternity
to deal the like to him as well.
'The Church commands and bids us quell
our hate and pray for all our foes.'
I say I'm wrong and shamed: he fell
on me but under God who knows.

5

I'll pray for him and with a will
upon the soul of Jean Cotart.
But how? I'm slow at reading still.
In Picard prayers[3] I'll go so far.
He hasn't the faintest what these are
so he must trust I spread no slanders
or go before too late as far
to learn as Lille or Douai in Flanders.

6

However, he mustn't tell a soul
if he intends to hear my prayer.
I give my word that on the whole
he won't be disappointed there.
When there's a psalter going spare
(not hide- or cordovan-bound) why then
I'll make the seventh verse my prayer
from *Deus Laudem*[4] and amen.

7

Si prie au benoist fils de Dieu
Qu'a tous mes besoings je reclame,
Que ma povre priere ait lieu
Vers luy de qui tiens corps et ame,
Qui m'a preservé de maint blasme
Et franchy de ville puissance,
Loué soit il et Nostre Dame
Et Loÿs, le bon roy de France.

8

Auquel doint Dieu l'eur de Jacob
Et de Salmon l'onneur et gloire –
Quant de proesse, il en a trop,
De force aussi, par m'ame, voire ! –
En ce monde cy transsitoire,
Tant qu'il a de long ne de lé★
Affin que de luy soit memoire
Vivre autant que Mathusalé.

9

Et douze beaux enfans tous masles
Vëoir de son cher sang royal†
Aussi preux que fut le grant Charles,
Conceus en ventre nupcial,
Bons comme fut sainct Marcial.
Ainsi en preigne au feu Dauphin !
Je ne luy souhaitte autre mal,
Et puis Paradis en la fin.

★Longnon-Foulet reads 'Tant qu'il a de long et de lé'.
†Longnon-Foulet reads 'Voire de son chier sang royal'. Bonner reads
'Vëoir de son chier sang royal'. I follow Kinnell here.

7

And so I pray the Blessed Son
of God who hears my cries of need
that my poor prayer, all said and done,
find grace with Him from whom proceed
body and soul. For I was freed
from wretchedness and vile mischance
and more oppression by God's speed.
Praise Him – and the good King of France.[5]

8

God grant the King all Jacob's fortune,
the glory and honour of Solomon
(prowess he has in good proportion
and strength of his own to go upon)
and make him such a paragon
throughout the passing world, both near
and far. And so his fame live on,
grant him the years of Methuselah here.

9

And thus may twelve male children spring
in holy wedlock from his royal line,
and dauntless as great Charles our king,
brave as St Martial[6] was. In fine,
may all his troubles then be tiny
and so may all of these attend
upon the ex-dauphin in time
and Paradise await his end.

10

Pour ce que foible je me sens
Trop plus de biens que de santé,
Tant que je suis en mon plain sens –
Si peu que Dieu m'en a presté
Car d'autre ne l'ay emprunté –
J'ay ce testament tres estable
Faict, de derniere voulenté,
Seul pour tout et irrevocable.

11

Escript l'ay l'an soixante et ung
Lors que le roy me delivra*
De la dure prison de Mehun,
Et que vie me recouvra,
Dont suis, tant que mon cuer vivra,
Tenu vers luy m'humilier,
Ce que feray tant qu'il mourra.
Bienfait ne se doit oublier !

12

Or est vray qu'après plainz et pleurs
Et angoisseux gemissemens,
Après tristesses et douleurs,
Labeurs et griefz cheminemens,
Travail, mes lubres sentemens –
Esguisez comme une pelote –
M'ouvrit plus que tous les Commens
D'Averroÿs sur Aristote.

*Longnon-Foulet reads 'Lue le bon . . .' here. Again I accept Kinnell.

10

And yet, because my strength grows weak,
poorer in goods than in my health,
and while I have the wits to speak
(what few God gave my only wealth
for I've had none by loan or stealth)
I make this will and testament,
the last deposals of myself,
once and for all, my true intent:

11

Written in sixty one, the year
the King delivered me from jail,
the harsh Meung. When death was near
he gave me life. I shall not fail,
while my heart beats, to tell the tale,
humble myself before the King
and do so till his life shall fail.
Good deeds bear long remembering.

12

True, that after cries and tears,
and groans of anguish, after pain,
toil and grievous wandering years,
suffering (feelings that remain
as sharp as cottonwool) made plain
more things than Averroës could
in all his Commentaries to explain
what Aristotle understood.

13

Combien au plus fort de mes maulx*
En cheminant sans croix ne pille,
Dieu qui les pelerins d'Esmaus
Conforta, ce dit l'Evangille,
Me monstra une bonne ville
Et pourveue du don d'esperance;†
Combien que le pecheur soit ville,
Riens ne hayt que perseverance.

14

Je suis pecheur, je le sçay bien.
Pourtant ne veult pas Dieu ma mort,
Mais convertisse et vive en bien,
Et tout autre que pechié mort.
Combien qu'en pechié soye mort
Dieu vit et sa misericorde,
Se conscience me remort,
Par sa grace pardon m'accorde.

15

Et comme le noble Rommant
De la Rose dit et confesse
En son premier commencement
Qu'on doit jeune cuer en jeunesse
Quant on le voit viel en viellesse
Excuser, helas ! il dit voir;
Ceulx donc qui me font telle presse
En meurté ne me vouldroient veoir.

---

*Longnon–Foulet reads 'Combien qu'au . . .' Both Kinnell and Bonner read 'Combien au . . .' though differing in their punctuation.

†Longnon–Foulet reads 'Et pourveut . . .' Kinnell and Bonner read 'Et pourveue . . .'

13

Yet in the depths of my despair
without a penny to my name,
God, who so comforted the pair
of pilgrims to Emmaus, came
and showed me in my deepest shame
a good city filled with great hope.[7]
However vile I was in sin and blame
God hates but those who need more rope.

14

I am a sinner, I know full well
and yet my death is not God's will,
but my return to live and dwell
in goodness – and others like me still
bitten by sin and doing ill.
However much I die in sin,
God lives and his great mercy will
forgive me if remorse bites in.

15

Though in those lines right at the start,
the noble *Romance of the Rose*[8]
states that we should excuse young heart
its youth once we have seen it grows
older than old. It's true, God knows!
And that's the reason those that hound
me up and down do not propose
to let my ripe old age come round!

16

Se pour ma mort le bien publique
D'aucune chose vaulsist mieulx,
A mourir comme ung homme inique
Je me jujasse, ainsi m'aist Dieux.
Griefz ne faiz a jeunes n'a vieulx
Soie sur piez ou soie en biere.
Les mons ne bougent de leurs lieux
Pour ung povre, n'avant n'arriere.

17

Ou temps qu'Alixandre regna,
Ung homs nommé Diomedès
Devant luy on luy amena,
Engrillonné poulces et des
Comme ung larron, car il fut des
Escumeurs que voions courir.
Si fut mis devant ce cadès
Pour estre jugié a mourir.

18

L'empereur si l'araisonna:
'Pourquoi es tu larron en mer?'
L'autre responce luy donna,
'Pourquoi larron me faiz clamer?*
Pour ce qu'on me voit escumer
En une petiote fuste?
Se comme toy me peusse armer
Comme toy empereur je feusse.

---

*Longnon–Foulet reads 'Pourquoi larron me faiz nommer?' Bonner and
Kinnell give 'Pourquoi larron me faiz clamer?'

16

Now if my death would benefit
the common good, as God's my judge,
I would condemn myself for it
and die in sin. I bear no grudge
nor harm for young or old that trudge
the earth on foot or lodge below.
The mountain foot will never budge
for poor men, neither to nor fro.

17

In Alexander's reign a man,
Diomedes, was brought for trial
before the King and under ban
of death for being beyond denial
the pirate sailing in such style
his men had seen at sea. That's why,
fingers in screws, he stood awhile
to hear the sentence: he must die.

18

At once the Emperor put the case:
'Why are you a robber on the sea?'
The man answered in the first place:
'Why speak of robber and robbery?
It's just because your men could see
me sail my pirate cockleshell.
If I'd the arms you lead, I'd be
like you – an emperor as well.

19

'Mais que veux-tu? De ma fortune,
Contre que ne puis bonnement,
Qui si faulcement me fortune,
Me vient tout ce gouvernement.
Excusez moy aucunement
Et saichiez qu'en grant povreté –*
Ce mot se dit communement –
Ne gist pas grande loyauté.'

20

Quant l'empereur ot remiré
De Diomedès tout le dit,
'Ta fortune je te mueray
Mauvaise en bonne,' si luy dit;
Si fist il. Onc puis ne mesdit
A personne mais fut vray homme.
Valere pour vray le baudit,
Qui fut nommé le Grant a Romme.

21

Se Dieu m'eust donné rencontrer
Ung autre piteux Alixandre
Qui m'eust fait en bon eur entrer
Et lors qui m'eust veu condescendre
A mal, estre ars et mis en cendre
Jugié me feusse de ma voix.
Necessité fait gens mesprendre,
Et faim saillir le loup du bois.

*Longnon-Foulet keeps to the second person singular here.

19

'That's how it goes. The life I lead
has come of Fate against whose will
I cannot struggle and succeed.
She casts the lots and cheats me still.
Forgive me for whatever ill
I've done, and learn that beggary –
the common saying fits the bill –
creates so little loyalty.'

20

The Emperor had understood
Diomedes' defence and swore:
'I'll change your fate from bad to good.'
And did. Diomedes never more
maligned a man, but stood before
them all, honest and worthy too.
Valerian, 'The Great' in Roman lore,
vouches that this tale is true.

21

Had God allowed my path to cross
an Alexander who could feel
the pity to repair my loss
and I was once more seen to deal
in evil, then without appeal
I would condemn myself to the stake.
It's need that makes men rob and steal;
hunger makes wolves from forests break.

22

Je plains le temps de ma jeunesse
– Ouquel j'ay plus qu'autre gallé
Jusques a l'entree de viellesse –
Qui son partement m'a celé.
Il ne s'en est pié allé,
N'a cheval, helas. Comment don?
Soudainement s'en est vollé
Et ne m'a laissié quelque don.

23

Allé s'en est – et je demeure
Povre de sens et de savoir,
Triste, failly, plus noir que meure,
Qui n'ay ne cens, rente, n'avoir.
Des miens le mendre, je dis voir,
De me desavouer s'avance,
Oubliant naturel devoir –
Par faulte d'ung peu de chevance.

24

Si ne crains avoir despendu
Par friander ne par leschier.
Par trop amer n'ay riens vendu
Qu'amis me puissent reprouchier –
Au moins qui leur couste moult chier!
Je le dy et ne croy mesdire.
De ce je me puis revenchier:
Qui n'a mesfait ne le doit dire.

22

The days of youth I must regret.
I had my fling and more than most,
then came onset of age. And yet
behind my back they seemed to coast
away and not on foot or post –
astraddle, no. Vanishing !
All of a sudden gone like a ghost
and me stuck here without a thing.

23

All of them gone and I remain,
poor in my wits and wisdom, sad,
failing, blacker than blue; no gain,
no rents, no property I've had.
My least kin now (it's true, I add)
advance to disown me and forget
the ties of blood. They think it bad,
a lack of change, a length of debt.

24

I haven't spent it eating well
nor laying women, as they fear.
No excess love has made me sell
a thing to vex my friends with here –
nothing I mean that cost them dear !
On this at least I say, no less,
I'm innocent, my conscience clear.
Who does no wrong need not confess.

25

Bien est verté que j'ay amé
Et ameroie voulentiers,
Mais triste cuer, ventre affamé
Qui n'est rassasié au tiers
M'oste des amoureux sentiers.
Au fort, quelqu'ung s'en recompence
Qui est ramply sur les chantiers
Car la dance vient de la pance !

26

Hé, Dieu ! se j'eusse estudié
Ou temps de ma jeunesse folle
Et a bonnes meurs dedié
J'eusse maison et couche molle.
Mais quoi ? Je fuyoie l'escolle
Comme fait le mauvais enfant !
En escripvant ceste parolle
A peu que le cuer ne me fent.

27

Le dit du Saige trop luy feiz
Favorable – bien en puis mais –
Qui dit : 'Esjoÿs toy, mon filz,
En ton adolescence . . .' – Mais
Ailleurs sert bien d'ung autre mes,
Car : 'Jeunesse et adolescence' –
C'est son parler ne moins ne mais –
'Ne sont qu'abus et ignorance.' !

25

Yet it is true that I have loved
and gladly would again, but heart
turned sad and starving gut have shoved
me off the paths of love. My part
is someone else's for a start,
someone whose roast will reach the rafters,
who has the stomach for the tart.
The dance is one for larger grafters.

26

Hey, God! in the mad days of youth
if only I had used my head
and learnt how to behave in truth,
I'd have a house and a soft bed.
But like a naughty boy instead
I ran away from school. I make
these lines and soon as they are said
I feel my heart would almost break.

27

I took the Sage's words for truth
(much good it did me and to spare)
'Rejoice, oh young man, in thy youth.'[9]
But then again the words declare
another kettle of fish elsewhere:
'Childhood and youth,' to be precise,
no more no less his saying there:
'are vanity, ignorance and vice.'

28

Mes jours s'en sont allez errant
Comme, dit Job, d'une touaille
Font les filetz quant tisserant
En son poing tient ardente paille.
Lors s'il y a nul bout qui saille
Soudainement il le ravit.
Si ne crains plus que rien m'assaille
Car a la mort tout s'assouvit.

29

Ou sont les gracieux gallans
Que je suivoye ou temps jadis,
Si biens chantans, si bien parlans,
Si plaisans en faiz et en dis?
Les aucuns sont morts et roidis.
D'eulx n'est il plus riens maintenant.
Repos aient en paradis
Et Dieu saulve le remenant.

30

Et les autres sont devenus,
Dieu mercy, grans seigneurs et maistres.
Les autres mendient tous nus
Et pain ne voient qu'aux fenestres.
Les autres sont entrez en cloistres
De Celestins et de Chartreux,
Botez, housez, com pescheurs d'oistres.
Voyez l'estat divers d'entre eux !

28

My days[10] are swiftly spent like ends
the weaver trims off at a stroke
with a burning straw. A thread extends
a bit too far beyond the yoke
and goes up in a puff of smoke;
says Job. So I no longer fear
what twists and turns of fate provoke
for death's the level of all things here.

29

Where are the lads who cut a dash
I hung on to in earlier days,
in song so fine, in talk so flash,
so taking in their wit and ways?
Some are stark dead. No trace
of them remains. Oh, may they find
in Paradise their peace and place.
God save the others of my kind.

30

Now some of these for great lords pass,
thank God, and masters, too. But more
beg naked; see their bread through glass
in shops. And others long before
have entered in the cloister door:
Carthusians or Celestines,[11] no doubt,
and shod for oysterbeds on shore.
The wonder is how men turn out.

31

Aux grans maistres Dieu doint bien faire
Vivans en paix et en requoy.
En eulx il n'y a que refaire
Si s'en fait bon taire tout quoy.
Mais aux povres qui n'ont de quoy –
Comme moy – Dieu doint patience !
Aux autres ne fault qui ne quoy
Car assez ont pain et pitance.

32

Bons vins ont, souvent embrochiez;
Saulces; brouetz; et gros poissons;
Tartes; flans; oefz, fritz et pochiez,
Perdus et en toutes façons.
Pas ne ressemblent les maçons
Que servir fault a si grant peine.
Ilz ne veulent nuls eschançons,
De soy verser chascun se peine.

33

En cest incident me suis mis
Qui de riens ne sert a mon fait.
Je ne suis juge ne commis
Pour pugnir n'absoudre mesfait.
De tous suis le plus imparfait –
Loué soit le doulx Jhesu Crist ! –
Que par moy leur soit satisfait !
Ce que j'ay escript est escript.

31

God grant great men may do good works
and live the life of peace and quiet.
There's no correcting great men's quirks;
better to belt up than to riot.
The poor have nothing but disquiet,
like me. God grant a patient air!
The others have an ample diet:
rations and bread enough to spare.

32

Good wines they have and newly broached,
sauces and broths and great fat fish,
custards and tarts, eggs fried or poached
or scrambled – any way they wish.
Nor are they served with every dish
as masons like to be. With wine
they won't have things too waiterish
but pour and drink as they incline.

33

I've rather wandered off the track
on this digression. No judge to try,
nor one to punish, pardon, rack,
the most imperfect man am I.
Sweet Jesus Christ be praised on high!
And they, through me, the most hard-bitten,
accept his grace before they die.
What I have written, I have written.

34

– Laissons le moustier ou il est.
Parlons de chose plus plaisante.
Ceste matiere a tous ne plaist,
Ennuyeuse est et desplaisante.
Povreté, chagrine, dolente,
Tousjours, despiteuse et rebelle,
Dit quelque parolle cuisante.
S'elle n'ose, si la pense elle !

35

Povre je suis de ma jeunesse,
De povre et de petite extrace.
Mon pere n'eust oncq grant richesse,
Ne son ayeul nommé Orace.
Povreté tous nous suit et trace.
Sur les tombeaulx de mes ancestres –
Les ames desquelz Dieu embrasse –
On n'y voit couronnes ne ceptres.

36

De povreté me garmentant
Souventesfois me dit le cuer:
'Homme, ne te doulouse tant
Et ne demaine tel douleur
Se tu n'as tant qu'eust Jaques Cuer.
Mieulx vault vivre soubz gros bureau
Povre, qu'avoir esté seigneur
Et pourir soubz riche tombeau.'

34

Let's leave the Church much where it stands[12]
and talk of far more pleasant things.
No topic everyone expands
on, some it bores and some it brings
annoyance. Poverty always stings
(sad, peevish, lawless, full of spite)
with biting words and murmurings –
and if she daren't, she thinks all right.

35

From childhood onward I've been poor,
of poor and humble extraction come.
My father never had much store,
grandfather Horace no great sum.
Poverty hounds us from crumb to crumb.
On tombs where my ancestors lie
(God welcome them to Kingdom come!)
no crowns and sceptres catch the eye.

36

But often when I grouse how poor
my heart butts in and plainly says:
'Come off it, man, now don't deplore
so peevishly that you have less
than Jacques Coeur made.[13] Better to dress
in coarse homespun your skin and bone
than to have left a lord's largesse
and rot beneath the richest stone.'

37

'Qu'avoir esté seigneur . . .' Que dis?
Seigneur, lasse ! ne l'est il mais?*
Selon les davitiques dis
Son lieu ne congnoistras jamais.
Quant du surplus je m'en desmetz.
Il n'appartient a moy, pecheur.
Aux theologiens le remetz
Car c'est office de prescheur.

38

Si ne suis, bien le considere,
Filz d'ange portant dyademe
D'estoille ne d'autre sidere.
Mon pere est mort, Dieu en ait l'ame.
Quant est du corps il gist soubz lame.
J'entens que ma mere mourra,
El le scet bien, la povre femme,
Et le filz pas ne demourra.

39

Je congnois que povres et riches,
Sages et folz, prestres et laiz,
Nobles, villains, larges et chiches,
Petiz et grans, et beaulx et laiz,
Dames a rebrassez colletz,
De quelconque condicion,
Portans atours et bourreletz –
Mort saisit sans excepcion.

*Longnon–Foulet reads 'Seigneur, las ! et ne l'est il mais?'

37

To have been a lord? What have I said?
The lord's not what he was before.
In David's Psalms it may be read:
'His place shall know of him no more.'
As for the rest, it's not for poor
sinners like me to gloss the text,
but theologians. I leave it for
a preacher to tackle in his next.

38

I know I'm not, I quite agree,
an angel's son in an aureole
of stars and galaxies, not me.
My father's dead, God rest his soul,
his body in a stone-flagged hole.
My mother's dying, that I know
and she, poor woman, knows the whole.
Nor has her son so far to go.

39

I know that rich or poor, the wise
or foolish, parishioner or priest,
nobles or peasants, prince and miser,
high or low, beauty or beast,
ladies in high-turned collars, least
and last whatever their conception,
high hat or headscarf, west or east –
Death seizes all without exception.

40

Et meure Paris ou Helaine,
Quiconques meurt meurt a douleur
Telle qu'il pert vent et alaine.
Son fiel se creve sur son cuer,
Puis sue, Dieu scet quelle sueur !
Et n'est qui de ses maux l'alege,
Car enfant n'a, frere ne seur
Qui lors voulsist estre son plege.

41

La mort le fait fremir, pallir;
Le nez courber; les vaines tendre;
Le col enfler; la chair mollir;
Joinctes et nerfs croistre et estendre.
Corps femenin qui tant es tendre,
Poly, souef, si precieux,
Te fauldra il ces maux attendre?
– Oy, ou tout vif aller es cieulx !

42

BALLADE

Dictes moy ou, n'en quel pays,
Est Flora la belle Rommaine?
Archipiades ne Thaïs
Qui fut sa cousine germaine?
Echo parlant quant bruyt on maine
Dessus riviere ou sus estan
Qui beaulté ot trop plus qu'humaine?
Mais ou sont les neiges d'antan?

40

Though Paris dies and Helen dies,
whoever dies must die in pain:
a hollow in the breath that dries;
spleen bursts upon the heart to drain;
he sweats, my God, he sweats in vain.
For now no brother, sister, son
would take his place and bear that pain
moments before his life is done.

41

Death trembles him and bleeds him pale,
the nostrils pinch, the veins distend,
the neck is gorged, skin limp and frail.
Joints knot and sinews draw and rend.
O Woman's body, so suave and tender,
so trim and dear, must you arrive
at such an agony in the end?
Oh yes, or rise to Heaven live.

42

BALLADE

Now tell me where has Flora gone,[14]
the lovely Roman, her country's where?
Archipiades, Thais that shone,
her cousin once removed? And there
was Echo once, a trace on air,
by ponds and commons she would show
a beauty more than humans bear:
where is the drift of last year's snow?

Ou est la tres sage Helloïs
Pour qui chastré fut et puis moyne
Pierre Esbaillart a Saint Denis?
Pour son amour ot ceste essoyne.
Semblablement ou est la royne
Qui commanda que Buridan
Fust geté en ung sac en Seine?
Mais ou sont les neiges d'antan?

La royne blanche comme lis
Qui chantoit a voix de seraine?
Berte au grant pié, Bietris, Alis,
Haremburgis qui tint le Maine
Et Jehanne la bonne Lorraine
Qu'Englois brulerent a Rouan,
Ou sont ilz, ou, Vierge souvraine?
Mais ou sont les neiges d'antan?

Prince, n'enquerez de sepmaine
Ou elles sont, ne de cest an,
Qu'a ce reffrain ne vous remaine:
Mais ou sont les neiges d'antan?

43

AUTRE BALLADE

Qui plus, ou est le tiers, Calixte,
Dernier decedé de ce nom,
Qui quatre ans tint le papaliste?
Alphonce, le roy d'Arragon,
Le gracieux duc de Bourbon,
Et Artus le duc de Bretaigne,
Et Charles septiesme, le bon?
Mais ou est le preux Charlemaigne?

Where Heloise, whose wisdom shone,
whose love helped Abelard to bear
the gelding he had undergone
when sworn to vows a monk must swear?
And where now is that Queen so fair
who ordered them to sack and throw
Buridan in the Seine down there?
Where is the drift of last year's snow?

Where's Blanche the Queen, white as a swan,
her siren's voice upon the air?
Big-footed Bertha, Beatrice gone;
Alice, and Arembourg once heir
to Maine. Good Joan in Rouen square
burnt by the English. There they go,
but where, O Virgin, tell me where,
where is the drift of last year's snow?

Prince, do not ask in a fortnight where,
nor yet again in a year or so.
This is the burden of the air:
where is the drift of last year's snow?

43

ANOTHER BALLADE

And whereabouts is Callixtus the Third,[15]
the last to die descended in that name,
who reigned four years as pope? And what occurred
to Alphonse, King of Aragon, or became
of Bourbon's gracious Duke? I ask the same
of Arthur, duke of Brittany, and again
with Charles the Seventh of France with all his fame.
But where now is the greatest – Charlemagne?

Semblablement, le roy Scotiste
Qui demy face ot, ce dit on,
Vermeille comme une amatiste
Depuis le front jusqu'au menton?
Le roy de Chippre de renon,
Helas, et le bon roy d'Espaigne
Duquel je ne sçay pas le nom?
Mais ou est le preux Charlemaigne?

D'en plus parler je me desiste.
Le monde n'est qu'abusion.
Il n'est qui contre mort resiste
Ne qui treuve provision.
Encor fais une question:
Lancelot, le roy de Behaigne,
Ou est il? Ou est son tayon?
Mais ou est le preux Charlemaigne?

Ou est Claquin, le bon Breton?
Ou le conte Daulphin d'Auvergne
Et le bon feu duc d'Alençon?
Mais ou est le preux Charlemaigne?

44

AUTRE BALLADE

Car ou soit ly sains apostolles
D'aubes vestus, d'amys coeffez,
Qui ne saint fors saintes estolles
Dont par le col prent ly mauffez
De mal talent tout eschauffez,
Aussi bien meurt que cilz servans,
De ceste vie cy bouffez,
Autant en emporte ly vens.

What of the Scottish King of whom I heard
that half his face was red, or so they claim,
as amethyst from forehead to his beard?
The famous King of Cyprus, what a shame!
and there's that other one, now what's his name?
But I forget now – the good King of Spain!
Where are they gone, the mighty in their fame?
But where now is the greatest – Charlemagne?

I mustn't maunder on. It's so absurd.
The world is nothing but a cheating game.
None can resist death long but is interred
and none can make provision against its claim.
But just one further question all the same:
Ladislaus, King of Bohemia? Then again
where's his grandfather gone from whom he came?
But where now is the greatest – Charlemagne?

And Guesclin's where, that Breton knight of fame?
And Alençon, the brave Duke lately slain?
The Count of the Auvergne, Dauphin by name?
But where now is the greatest – Charlemagne?

44

ANOTHER BALLADE[16]

Now whether it's the Saintly Pope
robed in alb and amice, arrayed
in sacred stole and holy cope,
the one who in his anger laid
about the devil – he too must vade
like any knave within his pay.
One gust and light and life must fade:
that much the wind sweeps right away.

Voire, ou soit de Constantinobles
L'emperieres au poing dorez
Ou de France ly roy tres nobles
Sur tous autres roys decorez
Qui pour ly grans Dieux aourez
Bastist eglises et convens,
S'en son temps il fut honnorez
Autant en emporte ly vens.

Ou soit de Vienne et de Grenobles
Ly Dauphin, ly preux, ly senez;
Ou de Dijon, Salins et Doles
Ly sires et ly filz ainsnez,
Ou autant de leurs gens privez,
Heraulx, trompetes, poursuivans
Ont ilz bien bouté soubz le nez?
Autant en emporte ly vens.

Princes a mort sont destinez
Et tous autres qui sont vivans.
S'ilz en sont courciez n'ataynez
Autant en emporte ly vens.

45

Puis que papes, roys, filz de roys
Et conceus en ventres de roynes
Sont ensevelis mors et frois,
En autruy mains passent leurs regnes,
Moy, povre mercerot de Renes,
Mourray je pas? Oy, se Dieu plaist.
Mais que j'aye fait mes estrenes
Honneste mort ne me desplaist.

Constantinople's lord – whose grope
is golden-fisted – he must fade.
The King of France, noble past hope
of any other king, who made
convents and churches all arrayed
in awe of God's great name. It may
be honour in his time was paid:
that much the wind sweeps right away.

So too Grenoble's, Vienne's hope,
the Dauphin, so dashing and so staid;
or Doles, Dijon, Salins, the scope
of great men and the lines they made;
the same goes for the whole parade
of heralds, pages, in their pay –
they stuffed their mugs despite their trade:
that much the wind sweeps right away.

Princes for death are also made,
and everyone alive is fey.
Should this rouse anger, I'm afraid
that much the wind sweeps right away.

45

Since popes and kings and sons of kings
conceived in wombs of queens now lie
stone cold and buried underlings,
their crowns on other heads, won't I,
a poor pedlar from Rennes, just die?
Oh yes, if so it pleases God.
– An honest death would get me by
so long as I have shot my wad.

46

Ce monde n'est perpetuel
Quoy que pense riche pillart.
Tous sommes soubz mortel coutel.
Ce confort prens povre veillart
Lequel d'estre plaisant raillart
Ot le bruit lors que jeune estoit,
Qu'on tendroit a fol et paillart
Se viel a railler se mettoit.

47

Or luy convient il mendier
Car a ce force le contraint.
Regrete huy sa mort et hier,
Tristesse son cuer si estraint.
Se souvent n'estoit Dieu qu'il craint,
Il feroit ung orrible fait
Et advient qu'en ce Dieu enfraint
Et que luy mesmes se desfait.

48

Car s'en jeunesse il fut plaisant
Ores plus riens ne dit qui plaise.
Tousjours viel cinge est desplaisant,
Moue ne fait qui ne desplaise.
S'il se taist, affin qu'il complaise,★
Il est tenu pour fol recreu;
S'il parle, on luy dit qu'il se taise
Et qu'en son prunier n'as pas creu.

★Some texts repeat line 7 of this stanza as line 5 also. It makes poor sense, though, and I follow the Longnon-Foulet reading.

46

The world is no abiding place
whatever robber barons think.
All for the chopper in any case.
A comfort this upon the brink
for one who had when in the pink
of youth such wit. Now old and grey,
if he should give a nod and wink
they'd call it filth, senile decay.

47

And so he has to beg his keep.
Need drags him to this wandering.
Today, tomorrow, he begs for sleep
and death, heartsick with suffering.
And he would do a dreadful thing
but for the fear of God. As it stands
the old do break God's law and bring
about their end with their own hands.

48

For if when young he had a wit
no sally now can raise a smile.
His monkey face will never fit,
and every glance he gives is vile.
He shuts his trap to please awhile –
to all it seems senile decay.
He opens up – they hate his style.
His tree lacks plums they always say.

49

Aussi ces povres fameletes
Qui vielles sont et n'ont de quoy
Quant ilz voient ces pucelletes
Emprunter elles a requoy,
Ilz demandent a Dieu pourquoy
Si tost naquirent, n'a quel droit?
Nostre Seigneur se taist tout quoy
Car au tancer il le perdroit !

50

Les Regrets de la Belle Heaulmière

Advis m'est que j'oy regreter
La belle qui fut hëaulmiere
Soy jeune fille soushaitter
Et parler en telle maniere:
'Ha, vieillesse felonne et fiere,
Pourquoi m'as si tost abatue?
Qui me tient, qui, que ne me fiere,
Et qu'a ce coup je ne me tue?

51

'Tollu m'as la haulte franchise
Que beaulté m'avoit ordonné
Sur clers, marchans et gens d'Eglise;
Car lors il n'estoit homme né
Qui tout le sien ne m'eust donné
Quoy qu'il en fust des repentailles,
Mais que luy eusse habandonné
Ce que reffusent truandailles.

49

Like those poor crones who are so old
without a penny to call their own
when they see nubile girls of gold
nudging them off their pitch, they moan
to God and ask why they alone
were born before their time. Our Lord's
silent: he'd lose against a crone
like that in any war of words.

50

The Old Woman Regrets the Days of Her Youth

I heard the Lovely Armouress,[17]
as she was once so widely known,
complain in longing more or less
like this for youth again:
                    'You crone,
cat-thief and proud of it, you've thrown
me down and beaten me. But why?
Who cares if I split this bag of bones
and with the blow lie down and die?

51

'You've knocked me off the high horse
my beauty rode over merchants, clerks
and priests. In those days, of course,
a passing shadow of the darks
that I could light and the bright sparks
would give their one and all, and leave
remorse till later after the larks.
Nothing a beggar now would thieve.

52

'A maint homme l'ay reffusé –
Qui n'estoit a moy grant sagesse –
Pour l'amour d'ung garson rusé
Auquel j'en feiz grande largesse.
A qui que je feisse finesse,
Par m'ame, je l'amoye bien.
Or ne me faisoit que rudesse
Et ne m'amoit que pour le mien.

53

'Si ne me sceut tant detrayner,
Fouler aux piez, que ne l'aymasse
Et m'eust il fait les rains trayner
S'il m'eust dit que je le baisasse,
Que tous les maulx je n'oubliasse.
Le glouton de mal entechié
M'embrassoit – j'en suis bien plus grasse.
Que m'en rest il? Honte et pechié.

54

'Or est il mort, passé trente ans
Et je remains vielle, chenue.
Quant je pense, lasse, au bon temps,
Quelle fus, quelle devenue,
Quant me regarde toute nue
Et je me voys si tres changiee:
Povre, seiche, megre, menue,
Je suis presque toute enragiee.

52

'Yet I refused with most the men
(which wasn't very bright of me)
because I loved a fly boy then
and gave him all I had for free,
though sometimes going on the spree.
But, oh my Christ, I loved him well;
yet fast and loose he played with me
and only loved what I could sell.

53

'He could have dragged me through Shit Street,
trodden me underfoot, and still
I would have loved him. He could beat
me up and break my back at will,
I'd soon forgive him all the ill
if once he asked me for a kiss.
The filthy bastard took his fill:
shame and despair have come from this.

54

'But now he's dead these thirty years
while I survive grey-haired and old.
Oh, when I see what filth appears
when I am naked, I grow cold:
poor, dry, shrivelled, fold on fold.
What once I was, what now in age:
meagre and rank, nothing to hold –
I almost lose my mind in rage.

55

'Qu'est devenue ce front poly;
Cheveulx blons; ces sourcils voultiz;
Grant entroeil; ce regart joly,
Dont prenoie les plus soubtilz;
Ce beau nez droit grant ne petiz;
Ces petites joinctes oreilles;
Menton fourchu; cler vis traictiz,
Et ces belles levres vermeilles?

56

'Ces gentes espaulles menues;
Ces bras longs et ces mains traictisses;
Petiz tetins; hanches charnues,
Eslevees, propres, faictisses
A tenir amoureuses lisses;
Ces larges rains; ce sadinet
Assis sur grosses fermes cuisses
Dedens son petit jardinet?

57

'Le front ridé; les cheveux gris;
Les sourcils cheus; les yeulx estains,
Qui faisoient regars et ris
Dont mains meschans* furent attains;
Nez courbes de beaulté loingtains;
Oreilles pendantes, moussues;
Le vis pally, mort et destains;
Menton froncé; levres peaussues.

*Longnon–Foulet reads 'marchans' here.

55

'And where now has my smooth brow gone?
The arching eyebrows, the blonde hair?
The doe–like eyes whose glance could con
the canniest of men? And where
the fine proportioned nose; the pair
of intricate little ears; the chin
and dimple? My oval face so fair
with lovely lips and clearest skin?

56

'Long arms; the deft fingertips?
The lovely small–boned shoulders; neat
breasts and the full rondure of hips,
smooth and compact enough to seat
the tourneyings when lovers meet?
Where the broad loins and pursing cunt
centred in plump firm thighs, discreet
with a little garden out the front?

57

'My forehead's wrinkled, my hair grey,
my eyebrows thin, and sight grown dim
whose eyes once glanced and led my way
so many men. My ears once trim
hang down like moss, my face is grim,
colourless, dead, with furrowed chin,
nose far from beauty bent, a rim
of lips, fleshless as trod grapeskin.

58

'C'est d'umaine beaulté l'issue:
Les bras cours et les mains contraites;
Les epaulles toutes bossues;
Mamelles .... quoy? Toutes retraites,
Telles les hanches que les tetes;
Du sadinet, fy! Quant des cuisses,
Cuisses ne sont plus mais cuissetes,
Grivellees comme saulcisses.

59

'Ainsi le bon temps regretons
Entre nous, povres vielles sotes,
Assises bas, a crouppetons,
Tout en ung tas comme pelotes
A petit feu de chenevotes
Tost allumees, tost estaintes.
Et jadis fusmes si mignotes ...
Ainsi en prent a mains et maintes.'

60

BALLADE

'Or y pensez, belle Gantiere,
Qui m'escoliere souliez estre,
Et vous, Blanche la Savetiere,
Or est il temps de vous congnoistre:
Prenez a destre et a senestre.
N'espargnez homme, je vous prie!
Car vielles n'ont ne cours ne estre,
Ne que monnoye qu'on descrie.

58

'So this is human beauty's end:
arms writhed, crazed hands too weak to lift,
back hunched until the shoulders bend.
My breasts? No tits to nudge a shift;
my tail the same, skin all adrift.
My quim, for Christ's sake! And thighs?
No more than hafts, skin, bone and rift,
all blotched like sausages.[18] Some prize!

59

'That's how we regret the good times
among ourselves, peevish old fools,
squatting on our haunches in grime,
in grey heaps like balls of wool
around a hemp-stalk fire that cools.
The sooner flame, the sooner fall
of ash. We once were beautiful.
That's how it goes with one and all.'

60

BALLADE

So think it over, pretty Glover,[19]
my understudy once, and you,
Blanche, the Cobbler, take a lover.
Don't fuss for any man will do.
Think of yourselves before you're through.
Take right and left and down the line,
or like dud coins tucked in new
you'll have no currency or shine.

'Et vous, la gente Saulciciere,
Qui de dancier estre adestre;
Guillemete, la Tapiciere,
Ne mesprenez vers vostre maistre.
Tost vous fauldra clorre fenestre.
Quant deviendrez vielle, flestrie,
Plus ne servirez qu'ung viel prestre,
Ne que monnoye qu'on descrie.

'Jehanneton, la Chapperonniere,
Gardez qu'amy ne vous empestre;
Et Katherine, la Bourciere,
N'envoyez plus les hommes paistre.
Car qui belle n'est ne perpetre
Leur male grace mais leur rie.
Laide viellesse amour n'empestre,
Ne que monnoye qu'on descrie.

'Filles, vueillez vous entremettre
D'escouter pourquoy pleure et crie,
Pour ce que je ne me puis mettre,
Ne que monnoye qu'on descrie.'

61

Ceste leçon icy leur baille
La belle et bonne de jadis.
Bien dit ou mal, vaille que vaille.
Enregistrer j'ay faict ces dis
Par mon clerc Fremin l'estourdis,
Aussi rassis que je le pense estre.
S'il me desment je le mauldis.
Selon le clerc est deu le maistre!

And you, sweet, keeping under cover
the spicy meat, the dance you do
entrances most; and you're another,
Jill, so good on carpets, too:
don't take your master in for you
will have to shut up shop in time
and take on some old priest to screw;
you'll have no currency or shine.

Hat-trick Jean, don't let your lover
set his cap elsewhere. And you,
Kate Purseproud, you will surely suffer,
cock-teasing men with just the view.
Plain Jane gives a smile or two
but lovely sourpuss must decline.
In hideous age, with lovers few,
you'll have no currency or shine.

Girls for your own sake take my view.
Listen and learn how much I whine.
I cannot circulate; I'm through:
I have no currency or shine.

61

This lesson was given them to learn
by one once fine and beautiful.
Rightly or wrong, you may discern.
I've made Fremin[20] (whose brain's a bull
in a chinashop) give it in full.
I'm sound in mind as ever I'll be.
I'll curse him if he tries to pull
your leg. Clerks show the mastery!

62

Si aperçoy le grant dangier
Ouquel homme amoureux se boute.
Et qui me vouldroit laidangier
De ce mot en disant, 'Escoute:
Se d'amer t'estrange et reboute
Le barat de celles nommees
Tu fais une bien folle doubte
Car ce sont femmes diffamees.

63

'S'ilz n'ayment fors que pour l'argent
On ne les ayme que pour l'eure.
Rondement ayment toute gent
Et rient lors que bource pleure.
De celles cy n'est qui ne queure.
Mais en femmes d'onneur et nom,
Franc homme, se Dieu me sequeure,
Se doit emploier. Ailleurs, non!'

64

Je prens qu'aucun dye cecy
Si ne me contente il en rien.
En effect, il conclut ainsy –
Et je le cuide entendre bien –
Qu'on doit amer en lieu de bien.
Assavoir mon se ces filletes
Qu'on parolles toute jour je tien
Ne furent ilz femmes honnestes?

62

The man in love must face in this
a great danger, that's clear to see.
To some these words will come amiss.
They'll tell me: 'Listen here to me.
If love has given you a flea
in the ear, you're the one to blame.
Your fear is crass stupidity
for these were women on the game.

63

'If they just love to lay cash down
you only love them for your time.
They love at large men about town;
they laugh when purses weep, and climb
in bed with anything that's prime.
Women there are of faith and honour
where a decent man should pass his time
(so help me God!) or he's a goner.'

64

It makes me sad to hear this said,
and to imagine talk like that.
For he concludes upon this head
(I see what he is driving at!)
that one should love and hang one's hat
in spots of virtue. But I suggest
the girls I stop to have a chat
were once as honest as the rest.

65

Honnestes si furent vraiement
Sans avoir reproches ne blasmes.
Si est vray qu'au commencement
Une chascune de ces femmes
Lors prindrent, ains qu'eussent diffames,
L'une ung clerc, ung lay, l'autre ung moine,
Pour estaindre d'amours les flammes
Plus chauldes que feu saint Antoine.

66

Or firent selon le Decret
Leurs amys – et bien y appert.
Ilz amoient en lieu secret
Car autre d'eulx n'y avoit part.
Toutesfois, celle amour se part*
Car celle qui n'en amoit qu'un
De celuy s'eslongne et despart
Et aime mieulx amer chascun.

67

Qui les meut a ce? J'ymagine –
Sans l'onneur des dames blasmer –
Que c'est nature femenine
Qui tout vivement veult amer.
Autre chose n'y sçay rimer,
Fors qu'on dit a Rains et a Troys,
Voire a l'Isle et a Saint Omer:
Que six ouvriers font plus que trois.

*Longnon-Foulet reads 'ceste amour' here.

65

Yes, and really honest, I mean,
without a spot of blame, though true
that when they came upon the scene
each took before they reached the stew,
a cleric, one; a layman, two;
a third some monk and served their turn
to quell the fires of love that grew
fiercer than St Antony's can burn.

66

It's clear their lovers all obeyed
the words of the decree: they lay
in secret – love no others made.
But soon their love was given away
for she who has one part to play
gets bored with it and soon has done.
From then she much prefers to stray
and make a play for everyone.

67

What drives them to it? I suppose,
without maligning woman's honour,
that from her nature clearly shows
the wish to have all men upon her.
I cannot rhyme the rest I ponder.
At Rheims or Troyes they all agree –
in Lille, St Omer, where you wander –
six navvies do more work than three.

68

Or ont ces folz amans le bont
Et les dames prins la vollee.
C'est le droit loyer qu'amans ont:
Toute foy y est viollee
Quelque doulx baisier n'acollee.
'De chiens, d'oyseaulx, d'armes, d'amours,'
Chascun le dit a la vollee:
'Pour ung plaisir mille doulours.'

69

DOUBLE BALLADE

Pour ce amez tant que vouldrez,
Suyvez assemblees et festes,
En la fin ja mieulx n'en vauldrez
Et n'y romperez que vos testes.
Folles amours font les gens bestes,
Salmon en ydolatria,
Samson en perdit ses lunetes:
Bien est eureux qui riens n'y a.

Orpheüs, le doux menestrier,
Jouant de fleustes et musetes,
En fut en dangier d'un murtrier
Chien Cerberus a quatre testes.
Et Narcisus, le bel honnestes,
En ung parfont puis se noya
Pour l'amour de ses amouretes.
Bien est eureux qui riens n'y a.

68

So foolish lovers take a knock,
their women take a broadside volley.
The only law in lovers' stock:
all faithfulness is merely folly,
however good the kiss, the dolly.
'In hawks and hounds, in love and war,'
everyone says the melancholy:
'one joy per hundred pains or more.'

69

DOUBLE BALLADE[21]

So take your fill of love and go
to banquets, feasts and festivals.
You'll have so little left to show.
The only thing you'll bang's your skulls.
Love calls the beast out where it stalls.
Solomon turned to idols in the fit.
and Samson lost sight of his balls:
Happy the man who has none of it.

Orpheus, gentle minstrel, though,
playing his flutes in dying falls,
for love came face to face below
with four-headed Cerberus who snarls;
Narcissus, honest fellow, spoils
himself and drowns to kiss the spit
image of all his loving girls:
happy the man who has none of it.

Sardana, le preux chevalier,
Qui conquist le regne de Cretes,
En voulut devenir moullier
Et filler entre pucelletes.
David, le roy, sage prophetes,
Crainte de Dieu en oublia,
Voyant laver cuisses bien faites.
Bien est eureux qui riens n'y a.

Amon en voult deshonnourer –
Faignant de menger tarteletes –
Sa seur Thamar et desflourer –
Qui fut inceste deshonnestes.
Herodes – pas ne sont sornetes –
Saint Jehan Baptiste en decola
Pour dances, saulx et chansonnetes.
Bien est eureux qui rien n'y a.

De moy, povre, je vueil parler.
J'en fus batu comme a ru telles,
Tout nu, ja ne le quier celer.
Qui me feist maschier ces groselles
Fors Katherine de Vausselles?
Noel le tiers est qui fut la.
Mitaines a ces nopces telles.
Bien est eureux qui rien n'y a.

Mais que ce jeune bacheler
Laissast ces jeunes bacheletes?
Non, et le deust on vif brusler
Comme ung chevaucheur d'escouvetes.
Plus doulces luy sont que civetes.
Mais toutesfoys fol s'y fya,
Soient blanches, soient brunetes.
Bien est eureux qui riens n'y a.

Sardana, the knight to overthrow
the realm of Crete, liked yarns and balls
and wished to spin with girls and sew.
David, the King and prophet, lulls
his fear of God for it and falls
for bathing thighs compact and fit –
the woman washing in the pools:
happy the man who has none of it.

Ammon it gave the wish to know
(pretending tart the point of calls)
his sister Tamar. He laid her low
which was incestuous and false.
No joke either when Herod feels
St John's head quits his favourite
for dancing jig and snatch in veils:
happy the man who has none of it.

Of me, poor me, you now must know.
How I was thrashed like laundry, balls
naked. I see no need just now
to keep it dark. Catherine de Vauselles
it was that made me bear such brawls.
For Noel there, a similar hit
upon the night his wedding falls:
happy the man who has none of it.[22]

You'd think the randy fellow, though
would leave the easy lays and dolls?
Not even if burnt like men that go
upon a broomstick. Sweetness he smells
subtler than civet. Whatever falls
a man is mad to trust a bit,
blonde or brunette; they make us fools.
Happy the man who has none of it.

70

Se celle que jadis servoie
De si bon cuer et loyaument
Dont tant de maulx et griefz j'avoie
Et souffroie tant de torment
Se dit m'eust au commencement
Sa voulenté (mais nennil, las)
J'eusse mis paine aucunement
De moy retraire de ses las.

71

Quoy que je luy voulsisse dire
Elle estoit preste d'escouter
Sans m'accorder ne contredire.
Qui plus, me souffroit acouter
Joignant d'elle, pres sacouter,*
Et ainsi m'aloit amusant
Et me souffroit tout raconter.
Mais ce n'estoit qu'en m'abusant.

72

Abusé m'a et fait entendre
Tousjours d'ung que ce fust ung aultre:
De farine que ce fust cendre;
D'ung mortier ung chappeau de faultre;
De viel machefer que fust peaultre;
D'ambesars que ce fussent ternes –
Tousjours trompeur autruy enjaultre
Et rent vecies pour lanternes –

*Longnon-Foulet reads 'm'accouter'. I follow Bonner here.

70

If she whom once I used to serve
freely and faithfully – who brought
me so much torment, broke my nerve
and tortured me – had only thought
to say she merely wanted sport
when first we met (no mention, none !)
I might have ducked the net she caught
me with and had a little fun.

71

No matter what I wanted to say
she always seemed quite keen to hear
without agreeing or giving way.
She'd even let me draw so near
we touched as I whispered in her ear.
But she kept stringing me along
and let me make my love quite clear
only to laugh and do me wrong.

72

Fooled me she did good and proper
that everything was otherwise:
flour was ash and clinker copper
and judge's hats were felt. Her dice
made snake's eyes double trey. Her eyes
said butter wouldn't melt in her mouth.
Liars accept each other's lies:
the moon is cheese and north is south,

73

Du ciel une poille d'arain;
Des nues une peau de veau;
Du matin qu'estoit le serain;
D'ung trongnon de chou ung naveau;
D'orde cervoise vin nouveau;
D'une truie ung molin a vent,
Et d'une hart ung escheveau,
D'ung gras abbé ung poursuyvant.

74

Ainsi m'ont Amours abusé
Et pourmené de l'uys au pesle.
Je croy qu'homme n'est si rusé,
Fust fin comme argent de coepelle,
Qui n'y laissast linge, drappelle,
Mais qu'il fust ainsi manyé
Comme moy qui partout m'appelle
L'amant remys et regnyé.

75

Je regnie amours et despite
Et deffie a feu et a sang.
Mort par elles me precipite
Et ne leur en chault pas d'ung blanc.
Ma vïelle ay mys soubz le banc.
Amans je ne suyvray jamais.
Se jadis je fus de leur ranc
Je desclare que n'en suis mais.

73

the sky a copper frying-pan,
and calfskin clouds water the crops;
and dusk was dawn when it began
and cabbage stumps were turnip tops,
and wine's best made from rotten hops;
a windmill is a war-machine,
a skein of yarn the noose that drops,
a portly priest, a soldier lean.

74

So love has made a fool of me
and run me out and locked the door.
No man has tricks enough, I see,
though mercurial his wits and more,
to come off lightly on this score
with even a rag to call his own.
Like me, he's beaten to the floor –
'The Reject Lover', I'm well-known.

75

Hereby all loves I do renounce
and curse, defy with blood and fire.
My death by them comes at a pounce,
and none of them thinks to inquire.
I've no time now to ease desire;
my fiddle's down behind the bench.
If ever in those ranks or higher,
I swear that I no longer wench.

76

Car j'ay mys le plumail au vent,
Or le suyve qui a attente.
De ce me tais doresnavant
Car poursuivre vueil entente.
Et s'aucun m'interroge ou tente
Comment d'amours j'ose mesdire,
Ceste parolle le contente:
'Qui meurt, a ses lois de tout dire.'!

77

Je congnois approcher ma seuf.
Je crache, blanc comme coton,
Jacoppins gros comme ung esteuf.
Qu'esse a dire? que Jehanneton
Plus ne me tient pour valeton
Mais pour ung viel usé roquart?
De viel porte voix et le ton
Et ne suys qu'ung jeune coquart.

78

Dieucy mer – et Tacque Thibault
Qui tant d'eaue froide m'a fait boire,
Mis en bas lieu, non pas en hault,
Mengier d'angoisse mainte poire,
Enferré. Quant j'en ay memoire
Je prie pour luy *et reliqua*
Que Dieu luy doint, et voire, voire,
Ce que je pense *et cetera*!

76

I've pressed my finger to the leak;
follow me if you like the spray.
I'll leave this topic now and speak
of what I started out to say.
If any ask me why the way
I speak of love is so unkind,
then let this saying win the day:
'A dying man may speak his mind.'

77

I feel the approaching of my thirst.
The gobs I hawk are cotton-white
and big as tennis balls that burst.
What more is there to say or write?
That Jill no longer likes the sight
of me, a broken-down old hack.
My voice is old and hoarse all right
but I'm still young and have the knack.

78

Thank God – and Tacque Thibaud[23] as well
who pumped me full of water neat,
quartered me underground in hell
and not above, who chained my feet
and gave me chokepears free to eat –[24]
I'll pray for him, *et reliqua*;
may God grant him, oh yes, complete,
what I've in mind, *et cetera*.

79

Toutesfois je n'y pense mal
Pour luy et pour son lieutenant,
Aussi pour son official
Qui est plaisant et advenant.
Que faire n'ay du remenant
Mais du petit maistre Robert.
Je les ayme tout d'ung tenant
Ainsi que fait Dieu le Lombart.

80

Si me souvient bien, Dieu mercis,
Que je feis a mon partement
Certains laiz, l'an cinquante six,
Qu'aucuns sans mon consentement
Voulurent nommer testament.
Leur plaisir fut, non pas le mien.*
Mais quoy? On dit communement
Qu'ung chascun n'est maistre du sien.

81

Pour les revoquer ne le dis
Et y courust toute ma terre.
De pitié ne suis refroidis
Envers le Bastart de la Barre.
Parmi ses trois gluons de fuerre
Je luy donne mes vieilles nates.
Bonnes seront pour tenir serre
Et soy soustenir sur les pates.

---

*Longnon-Foulet concludes this line 'et non le mien'. I follow Galway Kinnell here which seems the more colloquial. Bonner follows this reading but spells 'myen'.

79

And yet I bear him no ill-will,
nor his lieutenant,[25] and none;
not even his official, still
a pleasant, accommodating one.
Yet with the rest I swear I've done,
except for little master Rob.
I love them, every mother's son,
as God loves Lombards at their job.

80

Praise God that I remember well
certain bequests formerly framed
on my departure for a spell
in fifty-six. They have been named
The Testament by those who claimed
the pleasure which was never mine.
So what? It's commonly proclaimed:
'No man is master of his line.'

81

I don't mean to revoke all these,
though there my lands are all at stake.
Nor could my pity ever freeze
for Bastard of the Bar. I make
a gift of my old mats to shake
down with the strawbales on his floors.
He'll get to grips on those and take
a firmer stand upon all fours.

82

S'ainsi estoit qu'aucun n'eust pas
Receu le laiz que je luy mande
J'ordonne qu'après mon trespas
A mes hoirs en face demande.
Mais qui sont ils? S'on le demande:
Moreau, Provins, Robin Turgis.
De moy – dictes que je leur mande –
Ont eu jusqu'au lit ou je gis.

83

Somme, plus ne diray qu'ung mot,
Car commencer vueil a tester.
Devant mon clerc Fremin qui m'ot
S'il ne dort, je vueil protester
Que n'entens homme detester
En ceste presente ordonnance,
Et ne la vueil magnifester
Si non ou royaume de France.

84

Je sens mon cuer qui s'affoiblit
Et plus je ne puis papier.
Fremin, sié toy pres de mon lit
Que l'on ne me viengne espier.
Prens ancre tost, plume et papier.
Ce que nomme escry vistement,
Puys fay le partout coppier.
Et vecy le commancement:

82

If any legacies I left
have gone astray, I order now
that on my death the few bereft
should find my heirs and make a row.
In case you ask me who or how:
Moreau, Provins, Turgis,[26] I said,
and tell them straight: all mine, I vow,
is theirs down to this very bed.

83

In sum, I'll say just one more word
about it, then I must begin
my will. But first I want this heard
(my clerk Fremin will listen in
if he's not dozing off): herein
none shall be cut out of this will –
though I'd prefer no public din,
except in France a passing thrill.

84

I feel my heart is growing weak
and I can hardly say a thing.
Fremin, sit by my bed; I speak
so people cannot pry; and bring
pen, paper, ink. My murmuring
take down in haste, have copies sent
out everywhere. I'm opening
my last will and testament:

85

Ou nom de Dieu, Pere eternel,
Et du Filz que vierge parit –
Dieu au Pere coeternel –
Ensemble et le Saint Esperit
Qui sauva ce qu'Adam perit
Et du pery pare les cieulx –
Qui bien ce croit peu ne merit:
Gens mors estre faiz petiz dieux!

86

Mors estoient, et corps et ames
En dampnee perdicion;
Corps pourris et ames en flammes
De quelconque condicion.
Toutesfois, fais excepcion
Des patriarches et prophetes.
Car selon ma concepcion
Oncques n'eurent grant chault aux fesses!

87

Qui me diroit, 'Qui vous fait metre
Si tres avant ceste parolle
Qui n'estes en theologie maistre?
A vous est presumpcion folle.'
C'est de Jhesus la parabolle
Touchant du Riche ensevely
En feu non pas en couche molle,
Et du Ladre de dessus ly.

85

In the name of Eternal Father God,
and of his Son the Virgin bore
(Father eternal in our God),
and of the Holy Ghost who more
than saved all Adam lost before
and sends the damned to Heaven instead.
– You swallow that, your merit's poor:
bodies that turn to saints when dead!

86

Dead were they all, body and soul,
and damned to doom for ever more:
souls to the flames; to dust the whole
body, no matter what before.
I make exception on this score
for prophets and for patriarch,
who, as I see it, never bore
the pain of arse on heat and stark.

87

Though some will say, without a doubt,
'How dare you make remarks like these,
no theologian, you; it's out
and out presumption.'
                          A moment, please.
Jesus first made my point; he sees
Dives in Hell on no soft bed
while Lazarus who had no ease
has mounted high above his head.

88

Se du Ladre eust veu le doit ardre
Ja n'en eust requis refrigere,
N'au bout d'icelluy doit aherdre
Pour rafreschir sa maschouëre.
Pyons y feront mate chiere
Qui boyvent pourpoint et chemise
Puis que boiture y est si chiere.
Dieu nous en gart – bourde jus mise.

89

Ou nom de Dieu, comme j'ay dit,
Et de sa glorieuse Mere,
Sans pechié soit parfait ce dit
Par moy plus megre que chimere.
Se je n'ay eu fievre eufumere
Ce m'a fait divine clemence.
Mais d'autre dueil et perte amere
Je me tais et ainsi commence.

90

Premier: doue de ma povre ame★
La glorieuse Trinité
Et la commande a Nostre Dame,
Chambre de la divinité,
Priant toute la charité
Des dignes neuf Ordres des cieulx
Que par eulx soit ce don porté
Devant le Trosne precieux.

★Longnon-Foulet reads 'Premiere, je donne ma povre ame . . .' I follow
Galway Kinnell's version here which seems to be an emendation of
'Premier done de ma povre ame . . .' I prefer this version as it brings out
a typical Villonesque arrogant irony.

88

If Lazarus' finger had been hot
Dives would not have asked to feel
its coolness, nor to taste the spot
of water at its tip to heal
his burning throat. Guzzlers who peel
off coat and shirt for booze when broke
would not do well down there for real.
God save us all – and that's no joke.

89

Now, in God's name, as I've just said,
and of his Glorious Mother, I pray
to finish off the work ahead
without more sin from me. I may
be ghostly thin and yet I say
cholera missed me by God's grace.
My other ills must now give way;
it's time to start in any case:

90

First, my poor soul I now restore
to the blessed Trinity, consign
it to our Lady who once bore
our Lord, and pray that Heaven's Nine
Worthy Orders may incline
themselves in all their charity
and make this presentation of mine
before the precious throne for me.

91

Item: mon corps j'ordonne et laisse
A nostre grant mere la terre.
Les vers n'y trouveront grant gresse,
Trop luy a fait fain dure guerre.
Or luy soit delivré grant erre.
De terre vint; en terre tourne.
Toute chose se par trop n'erre
Voulentiers en son lieu retourne.

92

Item: et a mon plus que pere,
Maistre Guillaume de Villon,
Qui esté m'a plus doulx que mere
A enfant levé de maillon;
Degeté m'a de maint bouillon –
Et de cestuy pas ne s'esjoye,
Si luy requier a genouillon
Qu'il m'en laisse toute la joye –

93

Je luy donne ma librairie
Et le Rommant du Pet au Deable
Lequel maistre Guy Tabarie
Grossa – qui est homs veritable !
Par cayers est soubz une table.
Combien qu'il soit rudement fait
La matiere est si tres notable
Qu'elle amende tout le mesfait.

91

Item: I bequeath and leave my flesh
and bones to our great mother, earth.
The worms won't find it full or fresh
for hunger pinched its pennyworth.
Dispose it soon in its last berth.
From earth it yearned, to earth must yield.
Things always find their place on earth
if they don't wander far afield.

92

Item: to Guillaume Villon, more
than father to me, gentler far
than mother with her child; a score
of scrapes he's got me out of – bar
this last that gave him quite a jar –
I beg him on my knees to let
me well alone to make or mar
this mess for all the joy I'll get.

93

I leave my library for a start
to him – especially that work,
The Romance of the Devil's Fart,[27]
that Guy Tabary, an honest berk,
copied in notebooks which now lurk
beneath the table. A windy tale,
and yet the theme's enough to perk
the interest up should style fail.

94

Item: donne a ma povre mere
Pour saluer nostre Maistresse
– Qui pour moy ot douleur amere,
Dieu le scet, et mainte tristesse –
Autre chastel n'ay, ne fortresse
Ou me retraye corps et ame
Quant sur moy court malle destresse,
Ne ma mere, la povre femme:

95

BALLADE

Dame du ciel, regente terrienne,
Emperiere des infernaux palus,
Recevez moy, vostre humble chrestienne,
Que comprinse soye entre vos esleu,
Ce non obstant qu'oncques rien ne valus.
Les biens de vous, ma Dame et ma Maistresse,
Sont trop plus grans que ne suis pecheresse,
Sans lesquelz biens ame ne peut merir
N'avoir les cieulx. Je n'en suis jangleresse.
En ceste foy je vueil vivre et mourir.

A vostre Filz dictes que je suis sienne.
De luy soyent mes pechiez abolus;
Pardonne moy comme a l'Egipcienne
Ou comme il feist au clerc Theophilus
Lequel par vous fut quitte et absolus
Combien qu'il eust au deable fait promesse.
Preservez moy de faire jamais ce,

94

Item: I bequeath my poor mother
a prayer to Mary, Mother of God.
So much, God knows, I made her suffer
and rode all over her rough-shod.
When troubles pursue and I plod,
I have no other houseroom here
where I may rest my soul and body,
nor has my mother, the poor dear.

95

BALLADE

Lady of Heaven, Regent of Earth,
Empress of the Marshes of Hell,
welcome a christian of little worth
among your chosen ones to dwell
although my merits don't compel.
My Lady and my Mistress, your grace
is greater than my sin. No face
shall look on Heaven – this is no lie –
unless your goodness cover their case.
In this faith I mean to live and die.

So tell your son that by his birth
and death, I'm his. May he dispel
my sin and pardon me on earth
like Mary of Egypt, or as they tell,
Theophilus[28] who chose to sell
his soul to Satan for his place
and was acquitted by your grace,

Vierge portant sans rompture encourir*
Le sacrement qu'on celebre a la messe:
En ceste foy je vueil vivre et mourir.

Femme je suis povrette et ancïenne
Qui rien ne sçay, oncques lettre ne lus.
Au moustier voy dont suis paroissienne
Paradis peint ou sont harpes et lus
Et ung enfer ou dampnez sont boullus.
L'ung me fait paour, l'autre joye et liesse.
La joye avoir me fay, haulte Deesse,
A qui pecheurs doivent tous recourir
Comblez de foy sans fainte ne paresse:
En ceste foy je vueil vivre et mourir.

Vous portastes, digne Vierge, princesse,
Iesus regnant qui n'a fin ne cesse,
Le Tout Puissant prenant nostre foiblesse
Laissa les cieulx et nous vint secourir,
Offrit a mort sa tres chiere jeunesse.
Nostre Seigneur tel est, tel le confesse:
En ceste foy je vueil vivre et mourir.

96

Item: m'amour, ma chiere Rose,
Ne luy laisse ne cuer ne foye.
Elle ameroit mieulx autre chose
Combien qu'elle ait assez monnoye.
Quoy? une grant bource de soye,
Plaine d'escuz, parfonde et large.
Mais pendu soit il, que je soye,
Qui luy laira escu ne targe.

*Longnon-Foulet reads 'rompure'.

Virgin who bore the Mass on High
save me from anything so base.
In this faith I mean to live and die.

A poor woman of little worth,
I'm ignorant, can't read or spell.
I see in church the heavenly mirth
of lutes and harps or the damned in Hell
boiling. One picture makes me well;
the second one I cannot face.
Give me that joy, Goddess of Grace
on whom all sinners at last rely
in no sham faith nor idle ways.
In this faith I mean to live and die.

Virgin, Princess, you bore, by grace
In you, Our Lord who reigns – though base,
Low he became and left his place,
Lord of All Power in Heaven on High,
Offering his youth to save our race.
Now is he Lord; I grant his case:
in this faith I mean to live and die.

96

Item: to my dearest Rose[29]
neither my heart nor lights I give.
She'd jump at something else, God knows!
although she makes enough to live.
How? With a purse acquisitive,
silken and full and deep and wide.
But hang me or the next to give
a head or tail to toss inside.

97

Car elle en a – sans moi – assez.
Mais de cela il ne m'en chault.
Mes plus grans dueilz en sont passez;
Plus n'en ay le croppion chault.
Si m'en desmetz aux hoirs Michault
Qui fut nommé le Bon Fouterre.
Priez pour luy, faictes ung sault.
A Saint Satur gist, soubz Sancerre.

98

Ce non obstant, pour m'acquitter
Envers amours plus qu'envers elle,
Car oncques n'y peuz acquester
D'espoir une seule estincelle –
Je ne sçay s'a tous si rebelle
A esté, ce m'est grant esmoy.
Mais, par sainte Marie la belle,
Je n'y voy que rire pour moy –

99

Ceste ballade luy envoye
Qui se termine tout par R.★
Qui luy portera? Que je voye . . .
Ce sera Pernet de la Barre,
Pourveu s'il rencontre en son erre
Ma damoiselle au nez tortu
Il luy dira sans plus enquerre:
'Orde paillarde, dont viens tu?'

★Galway Kinnell reads 'erre' for 'R', which clearly indicates the point
of the rhyme-scheme.

97

Even without me she gets enough;
such ploys no longer make me boil.
I'm finished with the sorry stuff.
I will not stand for further toil.
I cede my rights in her as spoil
to Michaux the Fearless Fucker's heirs.
Pray for him; take a jump right royal;
he lies at St Satur below Sancerre.

98

And yet to square myself with love
rather than her – (she never dropped
a hint, a handkerchief or glove.
I don't know if all men have copped
the cold shoulder, and haven't stopped
wondering about it yet you see,
but by St Mary's beauty, I opt
for one great belly laugh from me) –

99

I send her this ballade in 'O'.
Who'll give it her? Now let me see.
Why Perrenet of the Bar will go
only providing he'll agree
if he should meet while roaming free
my lady whose nose is out of joint
he'll say without ado for me:
'You slut, which way do you point?'

100

BALLADE

Faulse beauté qui tant me couste chier,
Rude en effect, ypocrite doulceur,
Amour dure plus que fer a maschier,
Nommer que puis, de ma desfaçon seur,
Cherme felon, la mort d'ung povre cuer,
Orgueil mussié qui gens met au mourir,
Yeulx san pitié, ne veult Droit de Rigueur
Sans empirer ung povre secourir?

Mieulx m'eust valu avoir esté serchier
Ailleurs secours. C'eust esté mon onneur.
Riens ne m'eust sceu lors de ce fait hachier.
Trotter m'en fault en fuyte et deshonneur.
Haro, haro ! le grant et le mineur!
Et qu'esse cy? Mourray sans coup ferir?
Ou Pitié veult, selon ceste teneur,
Sans empirer, ung povre secourir?

Vng temps viendra qui fera dessechier,
Jaunir, flestrir vostre espanye fleur.
Je m'en risse, se tant peusse maschier
Lors. Mais nennil, ce seroit donc foleur.
Viel je seray ; vous, laide, sans couleur.
Or beuvez fort, tant que ru peut courir.
Ne donnez pas a tous ceste douleur :
Sans empirer, ung povre secourir.*

---

*Some attempts have been made to see an acrostic VJJLLON in this verse. Lines beginning in the indefinite article are surprisingly rare in Villon so it is tempting but either the text is hopelessly corrupt or Villon gave up the effort. In fact he usually makes acrostics of the more usual spelling of his name.

BALLADE (TO HIS GIRL-FRIEND)

Fake beauty whose cost to me is real;
Rough were the facts, all sweetness was the show;
A love tougher on the teeth than steel,
Named now there's little more to undergo.
Charming your stealth that dealt my heart the blow;
One pride, your secret, was to cut men dead.
Your eyes are pitiless; won't Justice show
Some cure for man – no knock upon the head.

More worth my while it were to make appeal
Anywhere else, and honour keep; but no,
Really there's nothing lures me from her heel.
Take off I must with only shame to show.
Help me, help me, anyone, high or low!
Eh what? Or shall I die before I shed
a blow? Won't pity hear my cry and show
some cure for man – no knock upon the head.[30]

Toward your flower, blooming now, will steal
a time to wither, dry and fade the glow.
I'll laugh then if my jaws can make a meal
of it. But no; it would be madness – no!
Old then myself and you but an old crow.
So drink deep while freshets fill the bed
Don't mark them all with tortures I can show:
some cure for man – no knock upon the head.

Prince amoureux, des amans le greigneur,
Vostre mal gré ne vouldroye encourir
Mais tout franc cuer doit par Nostre Seigneur*
Sans empirer ung povre secourir.

101

Item: a maistre Ythier Marchant
Auquel mon branc laissai jadis
Donne, mais qu'il le mette en chant,
Ce lay contenant des vers dix,
Et, au luz, ung *De profundis*
Pour ses ancïennes amours
Desquelles le nom je ne dis
Car il me hairoit a tous jours.

102

LAY

Mort, j'appelle de ta rigueur,
Qui m'as ma maistresse ravie,
Et n'es pas encore assouvie
Se tu ne me tiens en langueur.

Oncques puis n'eus force, vigueur;
Mais que te nuysoit elle en vie?
Mort, j'appelle de ta rigueur,
Qui m'as ma maistresse ravie.

Deux estions et n'avions qu'ung cuer.
S'il est mort, force est que devie,
Voire, ou que je vive sans vie
Comme les images, par cuer.†

*Longnon-Foulet reads 'pour' for 'par' here.
†In this lay I follow Bonner's lay-out which seems clinched by the
setting he quotes in his notes. If the lines which repeat are counted once
only it still amounts to 'vers dix'. The normal lay-out amounts to twelve,
anyway, if you count the two occurrences of 'Mort' as single lines.

Prince of love whom lovers serve below,
don't shift your favour from me for what's said:
frank hearts should for our Saviour show
some cure for man – no knock upon the head.

IOI

Item: to Ythier Marchant[31] to whom
I left my sword not long before
I now bequeath ten lines of gloom
to which he must prepare a score
for lute and voice to mourn the more
his former girls: a *De Profundis*.
Their proper name I shall ignore
or he'd hate me for a month of Sundays.

IO2

LAY

Death, I appeal against your rigour.
My mistress you abduct and rape,
and from your urge none can escape:
you have embraced my nerveless figure.

Since then I've lost my nerve, my vigour.
What harmed you in her living?
Death, I appeal against your rigour,
my mistress you abduct and rape.

Though two, we lived in nothing bigger
than one heart: I can't escape
if it is dead; or I'll just gape
lifelessly live, a carved figure.

103

Item: a maistre Jehan Cornu
Autre nouveau laiz lui vueil faire
Car il m'a tous jours secouru
A mon grant besoing et affaire.
Pour çe, le jardin luy transfere
Que maistre Pierre Bobignon
M'arenta, en faisant refaire
L'uys et redrecier le pignon.

104

Par faulte d'ung uys j'y perdis
Ung grez et ung manche de houe.
Alors huit faulcons, non pas dix,
N'y eussent pas prins une aloue.
L'ostel est seur, mais qu'on le cloue.
Pour enseigne y mis ung havet.
Qui que l'ait prins, point ne m'en loue –
Sanglante nuyt et bas chevet !

105

Item: et pour ce que la femme
De maistre Pierre Saint Amant
(Combien, se coulpe y a a l'ame,
Dieu luy pardonne doulcement.)
Me mist ou renc de cayement,
Pour *le Cheval Blanc* qui ne bouge
Luy change a une jument
Et *la Mulle* a ung asne rouge.

103

Item: for master Jean Cornu[32]
I'd like to leave one more bequest
for he has always helped me through
in times of need and bitter test.
I give him then with all the rest
Bobignon's garden, rented me
provided I had the gable dressed
and fixed the door on tenancy.

104

Because that door was gone I lost
a hoe-shaft there and paving-stone.
Not eight, not even ten hawks tossed
inside could ever catch a lone
lark. Though if the bolt is thrown
the house is safe. I slung my hook
there as my sign but that has flown.
A hard and bloody night to the crook!

105

Item: and though the wife of master
Pierre St Amant[33] (if she's to blame
may God forgive her my disaster)
made me a beggar – all the same,
to *The White Horse* who's never game,
in part-exchange I give a mare;
and to *The She Mule*, hardly tame,
a red-hot ass that's going spare.

106

Item: donne a sire Denis
Hesselin, esleu de Paris,
Quatorze muys de vin d'Aulnis
Prins sur Turgis a mes perilz!
S'il en buvoit tant que peris
En fust son sens et sa raison,
Qu'on mette de l'eaue es barilz.
Vin pert mainte bonne maison.

107

Item: donne a mon advocat,
Maistre Guillaume Charruau,
Quoy que Marchant ot pour estat,*
Mon branc. Je me tais du fourreau.
Il aura avec ung rëau
En change affin que sa bource enfle
Prins sur la chaussee et carreau
De la grant cousture du Temple.

108

Item: mon procureur Fournier
Aura pour toutes ses corvees
(Simple sera de l'espargnier)
En ma bource quatre havees
Car maintes causes m'a sauvees –
Justes, ainsi Jhesu Christ m'aide!
Commes telles se sont trouvees.
Mais bon droit a bon mestier d'aide.

*Longnon-Foulet reads 'marchande' in this line. However, the context makes it clear that Villon refers to his old enemy Marchant.

106

Item: fourteen barrels of wine,
taken from Turgis, that I select
at my own risk, I would assign
Sire Dennis Hesselin,[34] Elect
of Paris. If he drinks unchecked
until his reason floods and drowns,
top up with water. For wine has wrecked
many fine houses in the towns.

107

Item: I give my lawyer my sword –
Guillaume Charruau – although
I left it last to Marchant. (No word
about the sheath!) A fartthing or so
he'll get in change and that will go
to bloat his purse, found in the square
or flag-stoned walks around the show-
place of the Templars – somewhere there!

108

Item: to Fournier,[35] my advocate,
for all the thankless tasks he's done
(this time my costs are moderate),
for all the cases he has won,
and justly, by God's only Son!
– four fistfuls of my purse, all-told.
Justice was done. Good cause there's none
unless the lawyer's good as gold.

109

Item: je donne a maistre Jaques
Raguier *le Grant Godet* de Greve
Pourveu qu'il paiera quatre plaques –
Deust il vendre quoy qu'il luy griefve
Ce dont on cueuvre mol et greve,
Aller sans chausses, en eschappin –
Se sans moy boit, assiet ne lieve,
Au trou de *la Pomme de Pin.*

110

Item: quant est de Merebeuf
Et de Nicolas de Louviers,
Vache ne leur donne ne beuf
Car vachiers ne sont ne bouviers
Mais gens a porter espreviers –
Ne cuidez pas que je me joue –
Et pour prendre perdris, plouviers,
Sans faillir, sur la Machecoue.

111

Item: viengne Robin Turgis
A moy, je luy paieray son vin.
Combien s'il treuve mon logis
Plus fort sera que le devin.
Le droit luy donne d'eschevin
Que j'ay comme enfant de Paris.
Se je parle ung peu poictevin
Ice m'ont deux dames apris.

109

Item: I leave *The Great Wine Cup*,
Place de Grève, to Master Jacques
Raguier[36] as long as he'll pay up
four plackets – though, to get his whack
he'll have to sell what hides the slack
from thigh to calf, and go bare–skin
in pumps, if he won't take his tack
and drink with me in *The Pine Cone Inn*.

110

As for Merbeuf and Louviers,[37]
I leave them neither bull nor cow
for they're no stockmen. More truly they
are men to carry hawks (now, now,
don't think this is a joke!) to bow
and stoop on partridges and plover,
without a failure anyhow –
at Madam Machecoue's and under cover.

111

Item: should Turgis come to me
I'll pay the draught drawn on his cellar.
To find my place he'll need to be
much sharper than a fortune-teller.
Parisian–born and city–dweller,
I'll give him my right of magistrate,
for if I sound a southern fellow
two women taught my tongue the trait.

112

Elles sont tres belles et gentes,
Demourans a Saint Generou
Pres Saint Julien de Voventes,
Marche de Bretaigne ou Poictou.
Mais i ne di proprement ou
Yquelles passent tous les jours.
M'arme, i ne seu mie si fou
Car i vueil celer mes amours.

113

Item: Jehan Raguier je donne,
Qui est sergent, voire des Douze,
Tant qu'il vivra, ainsi l'ordonne,
Tous les jours une tallemouse
Pour bouter et fourrer sa mouse,
Prinse a la table de Bailly;
A Maubué sa gorge arrouse
Car au mengier n'a pas failly.

114

Item: et au Prince des Sotz
Pour ung bon sot Michault du Four,
Qui a la fois dit de bons motz
Et chante bien 'Ma doulce amour!',
Je lui donne avec le bonjour.
Brief, mais qu'il fust ung peu en point
Il est ung droit sot de sejour
Et est plaisant ou il n'est point.

112

And both now live at St Generoux,
a charming and a pretty pair,
on the borders of Brittany-Poitou,
near St Julien de Vouvantes there.
But nobody is larnin' wheare
somever these ladies pass the day.
I baint so daaft I do decleare:
I like to 'ide my luves away.[38]

113

I give to Jean Raguier,
the sergeant of the Twelve, so long
as he shall live, a cheese soufflé,[39]
daily from Bailly's, good and strong,
to stuff his gob, then go along
to wet his whistle at the côte
de Maubué. Eating, right or wrong,
has never bested him, I note.

114

Item: I give the Prince of Fools,
Michault de Four[40] to make a pair;
he sometimes cracks a good one, drools
'My Sweetest Love' with quite a flair.
I give him good day and do declare
if he brushed things up a little bit,
he's fairly foolish when he's there,
and when he's not all there, a wit.

115

Item: aux Unze Vingtz Sergens
Donne (car leur fait est honneste
Et sont bonnes et doulces gens)
Denis Richier et Jehan Vallette,
A chascun une grant cornete
Pour pendre a leurs chappeaulx de faultres.
J'entens a ceulx a pié, hohete !
Car je n'ay que faire des autres.

116

De rechief, donne a Perrenet –
J'entens le Bastart de la Barre –
Pour ce qu'il est beau filz et net
En son escu, en lieu de barre,
Trois dez plombez, de bonne carre,
Et ung beau joly jeu de cartes.
Mais quoy? Son l'oyt vecir ne poirre,
En oultre aura les fievres quartes.

117

Item: ne vueil plus que Cholet
Dolle, tranche, douve ne boise,
Relie broc ne tonnelet,
Mais tous ses houstilz changier voise
A une espee lyonnoise
Et retiengne le hutinet.
Combien qu'il n'ayme bruyt ne noise,
Si luy plaist il ung tantinet.

115

Item: of the Two Hundred and Twenty
Sergeants,[41] because their work's so straight,
and since they are so good and gentle,
to Dennis Richier, Vallette, his mate:
a velvet chinstrap to take the weight
right off the feet. I mean, of course,
the ones on foot, for to this date,
I haven't dealt with those on horse.

116

I give to Perrenet,[42] once more,
the Bastard of the Bar, I mean,
– a cleancut fellow at the core –
to change the bar sinister seen
upon his arms, a markedly clean
new deck of cards; three loaded dice;
what else? And if he farts out lean
or loud, the quartern fever, twice!

117

Item: I wish Cholet[43] would stop
dovetailing, butting and pegging board,
his hooping jugs and kegs, and swap
his tools for a good Lyons sword.
His cooper's mallet he may hoard.
Although he hates to form and fit
it's true that of his own accord,
he likes to knock and bang a bit.

118

Item: je donne a Jehan le Lou,
Homme de bien et bon marchant,
Pour ce qu'il est linget et flou
Et que Cholet est mal serchant,
Ung beau petit chiennet couchant
Qui ne laira poullaille en voye.
Le long tabart est bien cachant
Pour les mussier, qu'on ne les voye.

119

Item: a l'Orfevre de Bois
Donne cent clouz, queues et testes,
De gingembre sarrazinois,
Non pas pour acouppler ses boetes
Mais pour conjoindre culz et coetes
Et couldre jambons et andoulles
Tant que le lait en monte aux tetes
Et le sang en devalle aux coulles.

120

Au cappitaine Jehan Riou,
Tant pour luy que pour ses archiers,
Je donne six hures de lou
Qui n'est pas vïande a porchiers,
Prinses a gros mastins de bouchiers
Et cuites en vin de buffet.
Pour mengier de ces morceaulx chiers
On en feroit bien ung malfait.

118

Item: to John the Wolf I give
(a splendid man in part-exchange!)
since he's too frail and thin to live,
and Cholet's hunting is so strange,
a fine little setter with the range
to keep the birds from taking wing.
To cover up I will arrange
for tabards cloaking everything.

119

Item: the Woodsmith[44] I will stock
with Moslem ginger, a hundred bits
with heads and tails; but not to lock
in box or jar, but ass-over-tits
to sew up eels and thighs of chits
and bloat the belly out so much
that nipples stand with milk, and fits
of blood descend to balls and crutch.

120

Item: to Captain Riou,[45] the same
as for his archers, I bequeath
the meat of six wolves' heads that came
from butchers' dogs, then left to seethe
in cooking wine, not fit to teeth
a swineherd on. To taste such prime
meat once, almost all men that breathe
would readily indulge in crime.

121

C'est vïande ung peu plus pesante
Que duvet n'est, plume, ne liege.
Elle est bonne a porter en tente
Ou pour user en quelque siege.
S'ilz estoient prins a un piege
Que ces mastins ne sceussent courre,
J'ordonne, moy qui suis son miege,
Que des peaulx, sur l'iver, se fourre.

122

Item: a Robinet Trascaille
Qui en service – c'est bien fait –
A pié ne va comme une caille
Mais sur roncin gras et reffait,
Je lui donne de mon buffet
Une jatte qu'emprunter n'ose.
Si aura mesnage parfait;
Plus ne luy failloit autre chose.

123

Item: donne a Perrot Girart,
Barbier juré du Bourg la Royne,
Deux bacins et ung coquemart
Puis qu'a gaignier met telle paine.
Des ans y a demie douzaine
Qu'en son hostel de cochons gras
M'apatella une sepmaine,
Tesmoing l'abesse de Pourras.

121

Though heavier, this kind of meat,
than feathers, cork or down, it's fit
for soldiers in the field to eat
and during siege it helps a bit.
If wolves were trapped, and dogs that split
the hunt, they'd make fur-linings in
his winter coat. I order it
as doctor just to save his skin.

122

Item: Robinet Trascaille[46] who rides
to work on a fat and hefty horse
(and mounts it well) but never strides
as would a quail – on him, I force
a dish he is too shy, of course,
to borrow from my little hob.
His household's made with this resource
and nothing's lacking for the job.

123

Item: I give Perrot Girart,
sworn barber of Bourg la Reine,
two bowls and a big-bellied jar
since he slaves to make ends meet again.
Six years ago it must be when
he forcefed me a week on fat
porkers in his private den.
The Abbess of Pourras[47] swears to that!

124

Item: aux Freres mendians;
Aux Devotes et aux Beguines,
Tant de Paris que d'Orleans;
Tant Turlupins que Turlupines,
De grasses souppes jacoppines
Et flans leur fais oblacion,
Et puis après soubz ces courtines
Parler de contemplacion.

125

Si ne suis je pas qui leur donne
Mais de tous enffans sont les meres
Et Dieu qui ainsi les guerdonne
Pour qui seuffrent paines ameres.
Il faut qu'ilz vivent, les beaulx peres,
Et mesmement ceulx de Paris.
S'ilz font plaisir a nos commeres
Ilz ayment ainsi leurs maris.

126

Quoy que maistre Jehan de Poullieu
En voulsist dire *et reliqua*
Contraint et en publique lieu
Honteusement s'en revoqua.
Maistre Jehan de Mehun s'en moqua
De leur façon, si fist Mathieu.
Mais on doit honnorer ce qu'a
Honnoré l'Eglise de Dieu.

124

Item: to the Mendicant Brothers,
Daughters of God and the Beguines
of Paris and Orleans, the others,
those male and female Turlupines,
I'll make oblation by all means
of good thick Jacobin soup and custard.
Then pros and cons behind the scenes
for contemplation may be mustered.

125

Don't look at me. I give them less
than any mother and mother's son,
or God who so awards success
on those who suffer for their fun.
These fine fathers, like everyone,
must live – and those of Paris, too.
They give our women a pleasant run
and prove their love to husbands true.

126

Though Jean de Poullieu had his say
on this, they forced him to retract
in public. Jean de Meung made play
of all their ploys when he attacked
as did Matheolus in his tract.
But we must honour and obey
everything and anything in fact
that's honoured by the Church today.

127

Si me soubmectz, leur serviteur,
En tout ce que puis faire et dire,
A les honnorer de bon cuer
Et obeïr sans contredire.
L'homme bien fol est d'en mesdire
Car soit a part ou en preschier
Ou ailleurs il ne fault pas dire,
Se gens sont pour eux revenchier.

128

Item : je donne a frere Baude,
Demourant en l'ostel des Carmes,
Portant chiere hardie et baude,
Une sallade et deux guysarmes
Que Detusca et ses gens d'armes
Ne lui riblent sa caige vert.
Viel est ; s'il ne se rent aux armes
C'est bien le deable de Vauvert.

129

Item : pour ce que le Scelleur
Maint estront de mouche a maschié
Donne, car homme est de valeur,
Son seau d'avantage crachié
Et qu'il ait le poulce escachié
Pour tout empreindre a une voye.
J'entens celuy de l'Eveschié.
Car les autres, Dieu les pourvoye.

127

So I, their servant, shall submit
myself in all I do or say
to honour them as they see fit
with open heart, and to obey
without back-chat in any way.
It's mad exposing their affairs
and better not to have your say.
Public or private, vengeance is theirs.

128

Item: to brother Baude who lives
among the Carmelites, so brash
and big he acts, I'd like to give
a helmet and two pikes to bash
de Tusca and his men if rash
enough to rob his bird's rib-cage.[48]
He's old; if his sword still cuts a dash
he is the devil of an age.

129

And since the Keeper of the Seal
has so much beedung now to chew
and is so worthy, let me deal
him out pre-spittled wax, a screw
to crush his thumb to help him do
imprint and sealing in one go.
The Bishop's Clerk shall have his due
and God treat all the others so.

130

Quant des auditeurs messeigneurs
Leur granche ilz auront lambroissee,
Et ceulx qui ont les culz rongneux
Chascun une chaire percee.
Mais qu'a la petite Macee
D'Orleans qui ot ma sainture
L'amende soit bien hault tauxee.
Elle est une mauvaise ordure.

131

Item: donne a maistre Françoys,
Promoteur, de la Vacquerie,
Ung hault gorgerin d'Escossoys
Toutesfois sans orfaverie
Car quant receut chevallerie
Il maugrea Dieu et saint George.
Parler n'en oit qui ne s'en rie
Comme enragié, a plaine gorge.

132

Item: a maistre Jehan Laurens
Qui a les povres yeulx si rouges
Pour le pechié de ses parens
Qui burent en barilz et courges,
Je donne l'envers de mes bouges
Pour tous les matins les torchier.
S'il fust arcevesque de Bourges
Du sendail eust, mais il est chier.

130

As for my lords the auditors,
I'll panel out their barns; on those
that suffer in the arse with sores
some seatless chairs I would dispose.
For Little Macée, one of the pro's
of Orleans who took my money belt,
a hefty fine may they impose.
The awful shit, she always smelt.

131

Item: for swearing by St George
and God when dubbed a knight, I'll fix
up de la Vacquarie with a gorget[49]
of simple Scottish make – for kicks,
since all who saw and heard his tricks
could never speak or think of it
without bursting out like lunatics
and laughing till their sides would split.

132

Because he has his parents' sin
of drinking kilderkin and cask,
I leave Jean Laurens now the thin
linings of my bags, and ask
that every morning he makes his task
to wipe his poor red eyes quite clear.
Archbishops of Bourges may use a mask
of silk – but that is very dear.

133

Item: a maistre Jehan Cotart,
Mon procureur en court d'Eglise,
Devoye environ ung patart,
Car a present bien m'en advise,
Quant chicaner me feist Denise
Disant que l'avoye mauldite.
Pour son ame qu'es cieulx soit mise
Ceste oroison j'ai cy escripte:

134

BALLADE

Pere Noé qui plantastes la vigne;
Vous aussi, Loth, qui beustes ou rochier
Par tel party qu'Amours, qui gens engigne,
De vos filles si vous feist approuchier –
Pas ne le dy pour le vous reprouchier;
Archetriclin qui bien sceustes cest art;
Tous trois vous pry que vous vueillez peschier*
L'ame du bon feu maistre Jehan Cotart.

Jadis extraict il fut de vostre ligne,
Luy qui buvoit du meilleur et plus chier
Et ne deust il avoir vaillant ung pigne.
Certes, sur tous, c'estoit ung bon archier.
On ne luy sceut pot des mains arrachier.
De bien boire ne fut oncques fetart.
Nobles seigneurs, ne souffrez empeschier
L'ame du bon feu maistre Jehan Cotart.

*Longnon-Foulet reads 'qu'o vous vueillez perchier'. I like Kinnell's
reading – it seems more typical of Villon.

133

Item: to master Jean Cotart,
my lawyer in the Church's Court,
(I owe him just a penny so far
I think, or something not far short
from when Denise once had me brought
before the law because, she said,
I had abused her) this prayer I've wrought
to rest his soul now he is dead:

134

BALLADE (AND PRAYER)

Our father Noah who planted the vine,
and you too, Lot, who drank in a cave
till love that makes men foolish swine
had you and your daughters misbehave
(I don't reproach you though it's grave!)
Architriclinus – a master you are –
I plead with all of you to save
the soul of my late Jean Cotart.

For he descended from your line:
the best he drank, could never save
a penny to spend. A mighty fine
guzzler he was; he'd never waive
his round; he laboured like a slave
and none could drag him from his jar.
Lords, do not bar his way but save
the soul of my late Jean Cotart.

Comme homme beu qui chancelle et trepigne
L'ay veu souvent, quant il s'alloit couchier,
Et une fois il se feist une bigne,
Bien m'en souvient, a l'estal d'ung bouchier.
Brief, on n'eust sceu en ce monde serchier
Meilleur pyon pour boire tost et tart.
Faictes entrer quant vous orrez huchier
L'ame du bon feu maistre Jehan Cotart.

Prince, il n'eust sceu jusqu'a terre crachier,
Tousjours crioit, 'Haro ! la gorge m'art !'
Et si ne sceust oncq sa seuf estanchier
L'ame du bon feu maistre Jehan Cotart.

135

Item: vueil que le jeune Merle
Desormais gouverne mon change,
Car de changier envys me mesle,
Pourveu que tousjours baille en change,
Soit a privé soit a estrange,
Pour trois escus six brettes targes,
Pour deux angelotz ung grant ange,
Car amans doivent estre larges.

136

Item: j'ay sceu en ce voyage
Que mes trois povres orphelins
Sont creus et deviennent en aage
Et n'ont pas testes de belins
Et qu'enfans d'icy a Salins
N'a mieulx sachans leur tour d'escolle.
Or, par l'ordre des Mathelins,
Telle jeunesse n'est pas folle.

A drunk, he'd reel and roll in wine,
I often noticed, as he'd brave
the way to bed. He cut it fine,
one night, I know, with a close shave
on a butcher's stall. No drunkard gave
me such delight in any bar.
Open the gates; you hear him rave –
the soul of my late Jean Cotart.

Prince, his spit wouldn't reach the paving.
He used to roar: 'My throat will char.'
A thirst that never quenched its craving:
the soul of my late Jean Cotart.

135

Item: I'd like young Merle to take
in hand my money-changing rôle.[50]
(I do it against my will) but make
this stipulation for the whole:
to friend and stranger he must dole
out two heads to a single tail,
two sheets for every wad or roll.
Lovers should live on liberal scale.

136

Item: while travelling, I found
my three poor orphans fully grown,
no muttonheads but fairly sound.
From here to Salins, no kids known
have learnt so well the lessons shown
and salted them away. I swear
by the order of Bedlamites, youth flown
like that is not a fool's affair.

137

Si vueil qu'ilz voisent a l'estude.
Ou? sur maistre Pierre Richier.
Le Donat est pour eulx trop rude;
Ja ne les y vueil empeschier.
Ilz sauront, je l'ayme plus chier,
Ave salus, tibi decus,
Sans plus grans lettres enserchier.
Tousjours n'ont pas clers l'au dessus.

138

Cecy estudient, et ho !
Plus proceder je leur deffens.
Quant d'entendre le grant *Credo*
Trop forte elle est pour telz enfans.
Mon long tabart en deux je fens.
Si vueil que la moitié s'en vende
Pour eulx en acheter des flans*
Car jeunesse est ung peu friande.

139

Et vueil qu'ilz soient informez
En meurs quoy que couste bature.
Chaperons auront enformez
Et les poulces sur la sainture,
Humbles a toute creature,
Disans, 'Han? Quoy? Il n'en est rien !'
Si diront gens, par adventure,
'Vecy enfans de lieu de bien.'

*Longnon-Foulet reads 'leur' for 'eulx'.

137

And now I'd like them finished off.
But where? Richier's not too hard;
the *Donatus* they'll never cough
up with. But nothing must retard
them, so they ought to make their yard:
Ave salus, tibi d'écus[51] – then stop!
All further study they must discard.
Scholars don't always reach the top.

138

They'll learn as much as this, then wo!
I must insist they end their stint.
Such innocents could never show
the great Credo[52] a single glint
of interest. I'll pay – by dint
of selling half my tabard split
in two – and stand them each a mint.
All youngsters like to have a bit.

139

Manners they must be taught although
a thrashing is the only way.
Their hoods must fit, their thumbs must go
into their belts and they must say
humbly to all they meet each day:
'Hm, what? Oh no, that's quite all right.'
Then some will say and well they may:
'Now that's what I would call polite.'

140

Item: et mes povres clerjons
Auxquelz mes tiltres resigné,
Beaulx enfans et droiz comme jons,
Les voyant m'en dessaisiné
Cens recevoir leur assigné –
Seur comme qui l'auroit en paulme
A ung certain jour consigné –
Sur l'ostel de Gueuldry Guillaume.

141

Quoy que jeunes et esbatans
Soient, en riens ne me desplaist.
Dedens trente ans ou quarante ans
Bien autres seront, se Dieu plaist.
Il fait mal qui ne leur complaist.
Ilz sont tres beaulx enfans et gens
Et qui les bat ne fiert, fol est
Car enfans si deviennent gens.

142

Les bources des Dix et Huit Clers
Auront. Je m'y vueil travaillier.
Pas ilz ne dorment comme loirs
Qui trois mois sont sans resveillier.
Au fort, triste est le sommeillier
Qui fait aisier jeune en jeunesse
Tant qu'en fin lui faille veillier
Quant reposer deust en viellesse.

140

Item: to those poor little clerks
I signed my titles to of late,
as straight as ramrods and bright sparks,
one look has dispossessed my state
and I renounce for them the wait
(as good as theirs in any case
consigned in court on such a date)
for rent on Guillaume Gueldry's place.

141

Although they're young and harum-scarum,
they don't upset me – boys will be boys.
Thirty-odd years if God will spare them
and they'll grow out of tricks and toys.
It's wrong to cut up rough, annoys
with children well-behaved and good.
The birch is what a fool employs;
children turn people as they should.

142

The Eighteen Clerks will pay their keep
with their own pensions. I'll work that out
myself for them since they won't sleep
like dormice hibernating. No doubt
how sorry is that sleeping bout
where youth finds ease in youth. It takes
such hold on them they do without
when old they need to rest their aches.

143

Si en escrips au collateur
Lettres semblables et pareilles.
Or prient pour leur bienfaicteur
Ou qu'on leur tire les oreilles.
Aucunes gens ont grans merveilles
Que tant m'encline vers ces deux.
Mais, foy que doy festes et veilles,
Oncques ne vy les meres d'eulx.

144

Item: donne a Michault Cul d'Oue
Et a sire Charlot Taranne
Cent solz (s'ilz demandent, 'Prins ou?'
Ne leur chaille: ilz vendront de manne)
Et unes houses de basanne,
Autant empeigne que semelle,
Pourveu qu'ilz me salueront Jehanne
Et autant une autre comme elle.

145

Item: au seigneur de Grigny
Auquel jadis laissay Vicestre
Je donne la tour de Billy
Pourveu s'uys y a ne fenestre
Qui soit ne debout ne en estre
Qu'il mette tres bien tout a point.
Face argent a destre et senestre;
Il m'en fault et il n'en a point.

143

And letters similar to these
I'll send the collator. Let them pray
for me, their benefactor, please.
But someone clip their ears if they
refuse. Some people think the way
I care for these is strange. I'll swear
at feast nor fast I never lay
an eye upon their mothers there.

144

Item: I give to Michault Culdoe,
and Sire Charlot Taranne as well,
a hundred sous. If they must know
how come, they needn't fret; it fell
like manna. And should they do as I tell,
a pair of sheepskin boots[53] with uppers
and soles: Jeanne and another belle
they'll have to take and groom their cruppers.

145

Item: I leave to Grigny's Lord
to whom I gave Bicêtre before,
the Billy Tower to be restored
where there's a window or a door
unfit to function any more.
He can afford to have it done.
To left and right let money pour.
I need the cash and he has none.

146

Item: a Thibault de la Garde
(Thibault? je mens; il a nom Jehan)
Que luy donray je, que ne perde?
– Assez ay perdu tout cest an.
Dieu y vueille pourveoir, amen ! –
Le Barillet, par m'ame, voire.
Genevoys est plus ancïen
Et a plus beau nez pour y boire.

147

Item: je donne a Basennier,
Notaire et greffier criminel,
De giroffle plain ung pannier
Prins sur maistre Jehan de Ruel;
Tant a Mautaint; tant a Rosnel,
Et avec ce don de giroffle,
Servir de cuer gent et ysnel
Le seigneur qui sert saint Cristofle,

148

Auquel ceste ballade donne
Pour sa dame, qui tous biens a.
S'amour ainsi tous ne guerdonne
Je ne m'esbaÿs de cela
Car au pas conquester l'ala,
Que tint Regnier, roy de Cecille,
Ou si bien fist et peu parla
Qu'onques Hector fist ne Troïlle:

146

Item: to Thibaud of the Guard
(Thibaud? That's cuckoo! Jean's the name)[54]
what shall I give that won't come hard?
Too thick and fast my losses came
this year. May God restore the same.
Amen! Good Lord, *The Keg of Wine*,
of course. Though Genevois has more claim
with his great age and nose for sign.

147

A basket full of cloves I leave
Basanier, the notary
and criminal clerk, that he may thieve
from Jean de Ruel, and equally
to Mautaint and Rosnel to see
that with a lowly swift accord
they serve this gift of cloves from me
to St Christopher's devoted lord.

148

I give him this ballade[55] to toast
his lady who has all the charms.
If love is not so fair to most,
no wonder, for by feat of arms
he won her in the lists' alarms,
that René King of Sicily held.
As Hector or Troilus won their palms
without a vaunt – so he excelled.

149

BALLADE

Au poinct du jour que l'esprevier's s'esbat,
Meu de plaisir et par noble coustume;
Bruit la maulvis et de joye s'esbat,
Reçoit son per et se joinct a sa plume;
Offrir vous vueil, a ce desir m'alume,
Ioyeusement ce qu'aux amans bon semble.
Sachiez qu'Amour l'escript en son volume
Et c'est la fin pour quoy sommes ensemble.

Dame serez de mon cuer sans debat,
Entierement, jusques mort me consume,
Lorier souef qui pour mon droit combat,
Olivier franc m'ostant toute amertume.
Raison ne veult que je desacoustume
Et en ce vueil avec elle m'assemble,
De vous servir, mais que m'y acoustume,
Et c'est la fin pour quoy sommes ensemble.

Et qui plus est, quant dueil sur moy s'embat
Par Fortune qui souvent si se fume
Vostre doulx oeil sa malice rabat
Ne mais ne mains que le vent fait la plume.
Si ne pers pas le graine que je sume
En vostre champ quant le fruit me ressemble.
Dieu m'ordonne que le fouÿsse et fume
Et c'est la fin pour quoy sommes ensemble.

Princesse, oyez ce que cy vous resume,
Que le mien cuer du vostre desassemble
Ja ne sera: tant de vous en presume
Et c'est la fin pour quoy sommes ensemble.

149

BALLADE

At break of day the falcon claps his wings
More from pleasure and custom than for flight;
Blackbird sings and dances for joy which brings
Right to his feathers the mate who loves the sight.
Oh, then I burn within to take delight
In you and give you what would please all lovers.
So know how love writes this on sheets of white:
Enjoy the end we reach between the covers.

Dear to my heart beyond all reasonings,
Entirely mine till death consumes my light;
Laurel so sweet you still my sufferings;
Olive so frank you end my bitter fight.
Reason would rear me into your delight;
Even my will agrees to keep us lovers,
to serve you as my customary right,
enjoy the end we reach between the covers.

And what is more, in all my sufferings,
under a fortune often angry, the light
of your soft look destroys her menacings,
no more, no less than wind blows smoke from sight.
I do not sow the seed in soil that's light
but in your fields my oats and not another's.
God wills I fork and fertilize it right:
enjoy the end we reach between the covers.

Princess, listen to what I now recite:
my heart shall never turn from you to others.
I won't have it. Nor yours from mine take flight:
enjoy the end we reach between the covers.

150

Item: a sire Jehan Perdrier
Riens, n'a Françoys, son secont frere.
Si m'ont voulu tous jours aidier
Et de leurs biens faire confrere,
Combien que Françoys, mon compere,
Langues cuisans, flambans et rouges –
My commandement, my priere –
Me recommenda fort a Bourges.

151

Si allé veoir en Taillevent
Ou chappitre de fricassure
Tout au long, derriere et devant,
Lequel n'en parle jus ne sure.
Mais Macquaire, je vous asseure,
A tout le poil cuisant ung deable
Affin qu'il sentist bon l'arsure,
Ce *recipe* m'escript, sans fable:

152

BALLADE

En realgar, en arcenic rochier,
En orpiment, en salpestre et chaulx vive,
En plomb boullant pour mieulx les esmorchier,
En suif et poix destrempez de lessive
Faicte d'estrons et de pissat de juifve,
En lavailles de jambes a meseaulx,
En racleure de piez et viels houseaulx,
En sang d'aspic et drogues venimeuses,
En fiel de loups, de regnars et blereaulx,
Soient frittes ces langues envieuses.

150

Item: to Sire Jean Perdrier, nix,
and to his younger brother Francis.
They always helped me in a fix
and shared their goods and took their chances
even although my partner Francis
half prayed, half ordered me to try
a dish in Bourges, one of his fancies:
raw tongue and searing hot and high!

151

So out I went and took a look
in Taillevent, the chapter there
on fricassees. I read the book,
the length and breadth and depth with care
but found no mention of the fare;
still, here's Macquaire's great recipe
(he devilled Satan in his hair).
I swear to you he gave it me:

152

BALLADE[56]

In arsenic and sulphurous and pure,
in orpiment, in quicklime and salt-petre.
in boiling lead (the way to kill or cure)
in pitch and soot soaking in lye and beaten
in turds and piss, the wash of leper's feet,
in toe-jam and the clods from soles of boots,
in viper's blood, poisonous drugs and shoots,
in bile of badgers, wolves and foxes, dried,
in frogspawn and the hash of squirming newts
may these envious tongues be fried and fried.

En cervelle de chat qui hayt peschier,
Noir, et si viel qu'il n'ait dent en gencive;
D'ung viel mastin qui vault bien aussi chier,
Tout enragié, en sa bave et salive;
En l'escume d'une mulle poussive,
Detrenchiee menu a bons ciseaulx;
En eaue ou ratz plongent groings et museaulx,
Raines, crappaulx et bestes dangereuses,
Serpens, lesars et telz nobles oyseaulx,
Soient frittes ces langues envieuses.

En sublimé, dangereux a touchier,
Et ou nombril d'une couleuvre vive;
En sang qu'on voit es palletes sechier
Sur ces barbiers quant plaine lune arrive,
Dont l'ung est noir, l'autre plus vert que cive;
En chancre et fix et en ces ors cuveaulx
Ou nourrisses essangent leur drappeaulx;
En petiz baings de filles amoureuses
(Qui ne m'entent n'a suivy les bordeaulx)
Soient frittes ces langues envieuses !

Prince, passez tous ces frians morceaulx,
S'estamine, sacs n'avez ou bluteaulx,
Parmy le fons d'unes brayes breneuses.
Mais, par avant, en estrons de pourceaulx
Soient frittes ces langues envieuses !

153

Item: a maistre Andry Courault
'Les Contrediz Franc Gontier' mande.
Quant du tirant seant en hault,
A cestuy la riens ne demande.
Le Saige ne veult que contende
Contre puissant povre homme las
Affin que ses fillez ne tende
Et qu'il ne trebuche en ses las.

In brains of blackest cat that can't endure
to fish – so old it has no teeth to eat;
and in the drool and drivel which I'm sure
will do of some old mastiff now dead-beat,
mad and foaming at the mouth; then heat
in lather from a wheezing mule when the brute's
diced with good sharp scissors; next dilute
with water where the rats have ducked both hide
and snout, where lizards, snakes and reptiles root,
may these envious tongues be fried and fried.

In sublimate dangerous to touch; then skewer
and stuff into a living snake made sweet
with blood dried in a barber's porringer,
like chives a blackish green, when the moon's complete,
in chancres and tumours cooked in bowls where sheets
and nappies soak for wet-nurses; or shoot
the lot in tubs used by the whoring beauties.
(If you are one who's never seen inside
a brothel you'll not guess the tub's true duties.)
May these envious tongues be fried and fried.

Prince, take all these tasty curried fruits
and if you lack a colander then shoot
the lot through dirty pants and wring till dried
but first in pigshit or any swinish brute's
may these envious tongues be fried and fried.

153

Item: for Andry Courault alone
Franc Gontier[57] I will refute.
I ask the tyrant on his throne
for nothing. The poor should not dispute,
the Sage has said, nor press his suite
against the great. They lay the lines
and spread the nets and run the shoot
to catch him in their own designs.

154

Gontier ne crains; il n'a nuls hommes
Et mieulx que moy n'est herité.
Mais en ce debat cy nous sommes
Car il loue sa povreté,
Estre povre yver et esté
Et a felicité repute
Ce que tiens a maleureté.
Lequel a tort? Or en discute:*

155

BALLADE

Sur mol duvet assis, ung gras chanoine,
Lez ung brasier en chambre bien natee,
A son costé gisant dame Sidoine,
Blanche, tendre, polie et attintee,
Boire ypocras a jour et a nuytee,
Rire, jouer, mignonner et baisier,
Et nu a nu pour mieulx des corps s'aisier,
Les vy tous deux, par ung trou de mortaise;
Lors je congneus que pour dueil appaisier
Il n'est tresor que de vivre a son aise.

Se Franc Gontier et sa compaigne Helaine
Eussent cest doulce vie hantee,
D'oignons, civotz qui causent forte alaine,
N'aconçassent une bise tostee !†
Tout leur mathon ne toute leur potee
Ne prise ung ail, je le dy sans noysier.
S'ilz se vantent couchier soubz le rosier,
Lequel vault mieulx? Lict costoyé de chaise?
Qu'en dites vous? Faut il a ce musier?
Il n'est tresor que de vivre a son aise.

*Longnon-Foulet reads 'dispute' for 'discute'.
†It also reads 'acontassent' for 'aconçassent'.

154

But Gontier I do not fear.
He has no men; he is the heir
to nothing more than me, so here
we are in argument, one where
he praises poverty as his share
to last the summer and winter long.
He sees all happiness right there
in pauperdom. Let's see who's wrong:

155

BALLADE

A plump canon lolled on pillows of down
beside a stove in a room well carpeted,
and Dame Sidoine lay there without her gown,
white and smooth and soft, with stylish head.
On hippocras all day and night they fed.
They laughed and toyed around, kissed and caressed;
and flesh to flesh for greater ease they pressed.
– I saw them through the keyhole, learnt from these
that for alleviating sorrow best
no treasure's quite like living at your ease.

If Gontier and Helen had got down
to lead a life as sweet as this was led
they wouldn't give a toss for junkets, brown
soups, shallots and onions on which they fed
till the breath stank. A diet, I'd have said,
not worth a clove of garlic. Then they rest
beneath a rose and proud of it! What's best?
A bed and bedside chair? Which, if you please?
What need is there to make a further test?
No treasure's quite like living at your ease.

De gros pain bis vivent, d'orge, d'avoine,
Et boivent eaue tout au long de l'anee.
Tous les oyseaulx d'icy en Babiloine
A tel escot une seule journee
Ne me tendroient, non une matinee !
Or s'esbate, de par Dieu, Franc Gontier,
Helaine o luy soubz le bel esglantier.
Se bien leur est, cause n'ay qu'il me poise.
Mais quoy que soit du laboureux mestier,
Il n'est tresor que de vivre a son aise.

Prince, jugiez, pour tost nous accorder.
Quant est de moy – mais qu'a nul ne desplaise –
Petit enfant j'ay oÿ recorder :
Il n'est tresor que de vivre a son aise.

156

Item : pour ce que scet sa Bible,
Ma damoiselle de Bruyeres,
Donne preschier hors l'Evangille
A elle et a ses bachelieres
Pour retraire ces villotieres
Qui ont le bec si affilé –
Mais que ce soit hors cymetieres,
Trop bien au Marchié au fillé.

157

BALLADE

Quoy qu'on tient belles langagieres,
Florentines, Veniciennes –
Assez pour estre messagieres –
Et mesmement les ancïennes,
Mais soient Lombardes, Rommaines,
Genevoises (a mes perilz)
Pimontoises, Savoisiennes,
Il n'est bon bec que de Paris.

They live on oaten bread that's coarse and brown
and drink the stream from breakfast-time till bed.
All birds from here to Babylon, up or down,
could never make me stick water and bread
a single day – a morning, I should have said!
My God! Let Gontier and Helen nest
beneath the wild rose tree. If that seems best
it's up to them. And though one partly sees
the dignity of labour and the rest –
no treasure's quite like living at your ease.

Prince, settle the question I suggest;
but as for me (not wishing to displease)
when I was young I often heard expressed:
no treasure's quite like living at your ease.

156

Item: because she knows her Bible,
my Lady of Bruyères,[58] I grant
her and her girls without a rival
the right to preach from any cant –
except the gospels – so their rant
may save whores sharp in tongue and voice.
Outside the graveyards, or it can't
be done; the Linen Market's choice.

157

BALLADE

Although they have the slickest patter,
Venetian girls and Florentines,
the crones as well, come to the matter,
ready enough as go-betweens;
though Lombards, Romans spill the beans
and Genoese – I'll risk it then! –
from Piedmont to Savoyard scenes
there is no tongue like Parisienne.

De tres beau parler tiennent chaieres,
Ce dit on, Neapolitaines,
Et sont tres bonnes caquetieres,
Allemandes et Pruciennes.
Soient Grecques, Egipciennes,
De Hongrie ou d'autre pays,
Espaignolles ou Cathelennes,
Il n'est bon bec que de Paris.

Brettes, Suysses, n'y sçavent guieres,
Gasconnes n'aussi Toulousaines.
De Petit Pont deux harengieres
Les concluront – et les Lorraines,
Engloises et Calaisiennes,
(Ay je beaucoup de lieux compris?)
Picardes de Valenciennes:
Il n'est bon bec que de Paris.

Prince, aux dames Parisiennes
De beau parler donnez le pris,
Quoy qu'on die d'Italiennes
Il n'est bon bec que de Paris.

158

Regarde m'en deux, trois, assises
Sur le bas du ply de leurs robes
En ces moustiers, en ces eglises.
Tire toy pres et ne te hobes.
Tu trouveras la que Macrobes
Oncques ne fist tels jugemens.
Entens! Quelque chose en desrobes.
Ce sont tous beaulx enseignemens.

In Naples they hold chairs in chatter
to teach them what the other means;
German and Prussian women natter;
and yet although they may be queans
of Egypt, Greece or Hungarian scenes
or fetch from other field or fen;
Spanish or Catalonian colleens,
there is no tongue like Parisienne.

Bretons and Swiss can only smatter
like Toulouse Jills and Gascon Jeans.
Fishwives of Petit Pond'd scatter
all the lot in making scenes –
and Calais girls and libertines
of England, (I've got around again!)
and Picard girls of Valence. It means
there is no tongue like Parisienne.

Prince, to Parisian colleens
award the gift of the gab again,
and never mind Italian queans:
there is no tongue like Parisienne.

158

Look at them in twos or threes
sitting on hems of their long gear
in churches or in monasteries.
Don't put them off, but draw quite near;
such judgments you will overhear
as Macrobius never dared to make.
The barest facts they make quite clear;
you'd learn a lesson you could take.

159

Item: et au mont de Montmartre
Qui est ung lieu moult ancïen
Je luy donne et adjoings le tertre
Qu'on dit le mont Valerien
Et, oultre plus, ung quartier d'an
Du pardon qu'apportay de Romme.
Si ira maint bon crestien
Voir l'abbaye ou il n'entre homme.

160

Item: varletz et chamberieres
De bons hostelz (riens ne me nuyt)
Feront tartes, flans et goyeres
Et grans ralias a myenuit –
Riens n'y font sept pintes ne huit –
Tant que gisent seigneur et dame.
Puis après, sans mener grant bruit,
Je leur ramentoy le jeu d'asne.

161

Item: et a filles de bien
Qui ont peres, meres et antes,
Par m'ame, je ne donne rien
Car j'ay tout donné aux servantes.
Si fussent ilz de peu contentes
Grant bien leur fissent mains loppins
Aux povres filles, entrementes★
Qu'ilz se perdent aux Jacoppins,

★Longnon-Foulet reads '(ennementes!)' instead of this.

159

Item: to Montmartre Mount, a place
that is an ancient monument,
I give, and lay upon its base,
Mount Valerian – and the unspent
quarter of pardon it's my intent
to bring from Rome – so many more
Christians will poke about and enter
an abbey no man has known before.

160

The chambermaids and serving men
from wealthy households (and why not?)
make good tarts, strong cheesecake, then
they have a ball upon the dot
of midnight. Eight pints on the trot
will hardly warm them up, while lord
and lady sleep. I'll teach the lot
a quiet game of asses scored.

161

Item: to wealthy girls who still
have fathers, mothers, aunts, by God,
I'll give them nothing in my will.
I've shot their servants such a wad.
They don't demand a lot: the odds
and ends would give a power of pleasure
to poor young maids that now a squad
of Jacobins pick about at leisure,

162

Aux Celestines et aux Chartreux.
Quoy que vie mainent estroite
Si ont ilz largement entre eulx
Dont povres filles ont souffrete.
Tesmoing Jaqueline et Perrete
Et Ysabeau qui dit, 'Enné!'
Puis qu'ilz en ont telle disette
A paine en seroit on damné.

163

Item: a la Grosse Margot,
Tres doulce face et pourtraicture,
Foy que doy *brulare bigod*!
Assez devote creature –
Je l'aime de propre nature
Et elle moy, la doulce sade –
Qui la trouvera d'aventure
Qu'on luy lise ceste ballade:

164

BALLADE

Se j'ayme et sers la belle de bon hait
M'en devez vous tenir ne vil ne sot?
Elle a en soy des biens a fin souhait.
Pour son amour sains bouclier et passot.
Quant viennent gens, je cours et happe ung pot,
Au vin m'en fuis sans demener grant bruit.
Je leur tens eaue, frommage, pain et fruit.
S'ilz paient bien, je leur dis, '*Bene stat,*
Retournez cy, quant vous serez en ruit,
En ce bordeau ou tenons nostre estat.'

162

Carthusians as well and Celestines,
who, even though the order's strict
usually dine beyond their means;
the girls get plates already licked.
Perrette and Jackie I have picked
and 'Christ-yes' Isabel to bear
witness to hungers they inflict.
Who's hellbound giving girls the fare?

163

Item: to Fat Margot who's so fair
of face and painted, as I see,
devoted as she is, I swear
I love her for herself and she
loves me the way I've got to be.
If you come across the dear sweet soul
upon your travels make her free
with this ballade and read the whole:

164

BALLADE

I love and serve my lady with a will,
but that's no reason you should call me mad.
For her, I'd hitch on sword and shield to kill.
She is the goods to please my every fad.
When customers arrive, I lightly pad
to bring in pots and wine. I serve them cheese
and fruit, and bread and water as they please
and say (depending on the tip I'm paid)
'Do call again and come here at your ease
in this whorehouse where we do a roaring trade.'

Mais adoncques il y a grant deshait
Quant sans argent s'en vient couchier Margot.
Veoir ne la puis, mon cuer a mort la hait.
Sa robe prens, demy saint et surcot
Si luy jure qu'il tendra pour l'escot.
Par les costés se prent, 'C'est Antecrist,'
Crie et jure par la mort Jhesucrist
Que non fera. Lors j'empoingne ung esclat.
Dessus son nez luy en fais ung script
En ce bordeau ou tenons nostre estat.

Puis paix se fait et me fait ung gros pet
Plus enflee qu'ung vlimeux escharbot.
Riant, m'assiet son poing sur mon sommet.
Gogo me dit et me fiert le jambot.
Tous deux yvres, dormons comme ung sabot
Et au resveil quant le ventre luy bruit
Monte sur moy que ne gaste son fruit.
Soubz elle geins, plus qu'un aiz me fait plat.
De paillarder tout elle me destruit
En ce bordeau ou tenons nostre estat.

Vent, gresle, gelle, j'ay mon pain cuit.
Ie suis paillart, la paillarde me suit.
Lequel vault mieux? Chascun bien s'entresuit.
L'ung vault l'autre – c'est a mau rat mau chat.
Ordure amons, ordure nous assuit.
Nous deffuyons onneur; il nous deffuit
En ce bordeau ou tenons nostre estat.

But then fine feelings end and turn to ill.
When she comes home without the cash, I'm had.
I cannot stand her, she has blood to spill.
I hate her, grab her belt, gown, shift and plaid
and swear I'll flog the lot and her to add
up for the loss of all the nightly fees.
But hands on hips she hollers if you please
how I am anti-Christ and won't get paid.
I grab a club and sign her, nose to knees,
in this whorehouse where we do a roaring trade.

We make peace then in bed. She takes my fill,
gorged like a dung-beetle, blows me a bad
and mighty poisonous fart. I fit her bill
she says, and laughing bangs my nob quite glad.
She thwacks my thigh and, after what we've had,
dead drunk we sleep like logs – and let the fleas.
Though when we stir her quim begins to tease.
She mounts; I groan beneath the weight – I'm splayed!
Her screwing soon will bring me to my knees
in this whorehouse where we do a roaring trade.

Vary the wind, come frost, I live in ease.
I am a fucker; she fucks as I please.
Layman or laity – no matter of degrees!
Layer on layer of onion overlaid,
Our filth we love and filths upon us seize;
Now we flee honour, honour from us flees
in this whorehouse where we do a roaring trade.

165

Item: a Marion l'Idolle
Et la grant Jehanne de Bretaigne
Donne tenir publique escolle
Ou l'escollier le maistre enseigne.
Lieu n'est ou ce marchié se tiengne
Si non a la grisle de Mehun.
De quoy je dis, 'Fy de l'enseigne
Puis que l'ouvraige est si commun.'

166

Item: et a Noel Jolis
Autre chose je ne luy donne
Fors plain poing d'osiers frez cueillis
En mon jardin. Je l'abandonne.
Chastoy est une belle aulmosne;
Ame n'en doit estre marry.
Unze vings coups luy en ordonne,
Livrez par la main de Henry.

167

Item: ne sçay qu'a l'Ostel Dieu
Donner, n'a povres hospitaulx.
Bourdes n'ont icy temps ne lieu
Car povres gens ont assez maulx.
Chascun leur envoye leurs aulx.
Les Mendians ont eu mon oye.
Au fort, ilz auront les os:
A menue gent menue monnoye.

165

Item: to the Idol Marion
and big Jean of Brittany
I give them leave to carry on
a school where all the mastery
is pupil power for a fee.
These studies go on everywhere
except the jail of Meung maybe.
To hell with signs; the trade's not rare.

166

Item: to Noel Jolis I lash
out, giving him only a birch
fresh from my garden. Without cash
I leave him now right in the lurch.
Chastisement according to the Church
makes a good alms. He shouldn't mind.
I order Henry gives the urchin
two hundred and twenty strokes behind.

167

Item: I don't know how to endow
the Hotel Dieu nor any poor
hospitals. No joking matter now,
it's not the place. The poor have more
than their fair share of ills in store.
Everyone's scraps are in their range.
Friars cooked my goose and left the poor
the bones. To little men small change.

168

Item: je donne a mon barbier
Qui se nomme Colin Galerne,
Pres voisin d'Angelot l'erbier,
Ung gros glasson (prins ou? en Marne)
Affin qu'a son ayse s'yverne.
De l'estomac le tiengne pres.
Se l'yver ainsi se gouverne
Il aura chault l'esté d'après.

169

Item: riens aux Enfans Trouvez.
Mais les perdus faut que consolle.
Si doivent estre retrouvez,
Par droit, sur Marion l'Idolle.
Une leçon de mon escolle
Leur liray qui ne dure guere:
Teste n'ayent dure ne folle;
Escoutent car c'est la derniere:

170

Beaulx enfans, vous perdez la plus
Belle rose de vo chappeau;
Mes clers pres prenans comme glus,
Se vous allez a Montpipeau
Ou a Rueil, gardez la peau,
Car pour s'esbatre en ces deux lieux,
Cuidant que vaulsist le rappeau,
Le perdit Colin de Cayeux.

168

Item: to Colin Galerne, my barber,
next to the herbalist Angelot's,
I give a great ice-block to harbour
in his bosom. From? The floes
of Marne. To last the winter snows
hug it against the guts; and so,
if winter long he holds the pose
next summer's heat won't make him glow.

169

Item: to Foundlings, sweet Fanny Adams.
The Lostlings need consoling more.
They turn up usually at Madam's,
at Marion the Idol's door.
A single lesson on this score
I'll read, and one that flies right past.
Blockheads they mustn't be, but pore
upon it since it is the last:

170

Fair children take care not to lose
the rose's bloom beneath your hat.
You clerks with fingers like some glues,
if it's Montpipeau you're aiming at,
or Rueil, don't risk your neck for that.
For knocking off on either job
and making an appeal too pat
Colin de Cayeux[59] lost his nob.

171

Ce n'est pas ung jeu de trois mailles
Ou va corps et peut estre l'ame.
Qui pert, riens n'y sont repentailles
Qu'on n'en meure a honte et diffame,
Et qui gaigne n'a pas a femme
Dido la royne de Cartage.
L'homme est donc bien fol et infame
Qui pour si peu couche tel gage.

172

Qu'ung chascun encore m'escoute.
On dit et il est verité
Que charterie se boit toute,
Au feu l'yver, au bois l'esté.
S'argent avez, il n'est enté,
Mais le despendez tost et viste !
Qui en voyez vous herité ?
Jamais mal acquest ne prouffite.

173

BALLADE

Car ou soies porteur de bulles,
Pipeur ou hasardeur de dez,
Tailleur de faulx coings et te brusles
Comme ceulx qui sont eschaudez,
Traistres parjurs de foy vuidez;
Soies larron, ravis ou pilles –
Ou en va l'acquest, qui cuidez ?
Tout aux tavernes et aux filles.

171

The game is hardly worth the candle:
body and sometimes soul it takes.
The loser dies in shame and scandal
no matter what repentance he makes.
And he who gets the lucky breaks
won't win the hand of Dido, Queen
of Carthage. The man's a fool who stakes
so great a prize to win a bean.

172

Now listen all of you: they say
the profits on the draught are spent
upon the drayman on the way,
in woods in summer, in winter bent
over a fire. No cash is lent –
all given, so lash out all you owe;
don't leave behind a single cent
for easy come is easy go.

173

BALLADE

Whether you counterfeit your brass
and end so oiled you boil and bake,
traitors whose credit wouldn't pass;
or peddle pardons; learn to shake
the loaded dice; or maybe take
to filching in and out of doors –
where does it go, the money you make?
All to the taverns and the whores.

Ryme, raille, cymballe, luttes,
Comme fol, fainctif, eshontez;
Farce, broulle, joue des fleustes;
Fais es villes et es citez
Farces, jeux et moralitez;
Gaigne au berlanc, au glic, aux quilles –
Aussi bien va, or escoutez,
Tout aux tavernes et aux filles.

De telz ordures te reculles,
Laboure, fauche champs et prez;
Sers et pense chevaux et mulles
S'aucunement tu n'es lettrez.
Assez auras, se prens en grez.
Mais se chanvre broyes ou tilles,
Ne tens ton labour qu'as ouvrez
Tout aux tavernes et aux filles.

Chausses, pourpoins esguilletez,
Robes, et toutes vos drappilles,
Ains que vous fassiez pis, portez
Tout aux tavernes et aux filles.

174

A vous parle, compaigns de galle,
Mal des ames et bien du corps.
Gardez vous tous de ce mau hasle
Qui noircist les gens quant sont mors.
Eschevez le, c'est ung mal mors.
Passez vous au mieulx que pourrez.
Et, pour Dieu, soiez tous recors
Qu'une fois viendra que mourrez.

Rhyme or rail or clash your brass,
like shameless fools that always fake;
mime, mum, or try some magic pass;
or if in towns and cities, make
miracles, mysteries, jigs; or take
a trick or two or skittle scores –
soon gained, soon gone! (You still awake?)
All to the taverns and the whores.

If depths like these are not your class,
then plough up fields or drive a rake;
or turn to doctoring horse and ass.
But only if you cannot take
to book and pen. A crust you'll make.
Yet if you've slaved at prison chores
you haven't lifted loot to take
all to the taverns and the whores.

Before you do much worse then, take
trousers and shoes and all that's yours,
gowns and the silks for your own sake
all to the taverns and the whores.

174

It's you I'm talking to, old friends,
sick in the soul, in body sound:
keep out of wind and sun that sends
men black and blue. Don't hang around,
its bite is bitter, you may be bound.
So do your best to pass things by.
For God's sake, bear in mind the sound:
There is a time for you to die.

175

Item: je donne aux Quinze Vings –
Qu'autant vauldroit nommer Trois Cens –
De Paris, non pas de Provins,
Car a eulx tenu je me sens,
Ilz auront, et je m'y consens,
Sans les estuys, mes grans lunettes
Pour mettre a part, aux Innocens,
Les gens de bien des deshonnestes.

176

Icy n'y a ne ris ne jeu.
Que leur valut avoir chevances,
N'en grans liz de parement jeu,
Engloutir vins en grosses pances,
Mener joye, festes et dances
Et de ce prest estre a toute heure?
Toutes faillent telles plaisances
Et la coulpe si en demeure.

177

Quant je considere ces testes
Entassees en ces charniers . . .
Tous furent maistres des requestes
Au moins de la Chambre aux Deniers
Ou tous furent portepanniers.
Autant puis l'ung que l'autre dire,
Car d'evesques ou lanterniers
Je n'y congnois rien a redire.

175

Item: I give the Fifteen Score[60]
(Three Hundred the name should be)
not those of Paris, Provins, for
I feel they have some claim on me:
they'll have my glasses, I agree,
so they can clearly tell the face
of good from bad in the cemetery
des Innocents. But not the case!

176

There is no play or laughter here.
What good was wealth to them, to lie
in great fourposters, and what cheer
their paunches big with wine, the high
days, feasts and balls, the standing by
for one more giddy whirl. They're gone,
all of the pleasures they could try;
the evil that they did lives on.

177

I think of all the skulls that pile
inside the charnel houses here:
past masters of requests awhile
in the Treasury at least; or mere
porters instead; no longer clear
which one is which. I cannot say
this was a bishop; this would appear
a lantern-maker in his day.

178

Et icelles qui s'enclinoient
Unes contre autres en leurs vies,
Desquelles les unes regnoient
Des autres craintes et servies,
La les voy toutes assouvies
Ensemble en ung tas peslemesle.
Seigneuries leur sont ravies:
Clerc ne maistre ne s'y appelle.

179

Or sont ilz mors, Dieu ait leur ames.
Quant est des corps, ilz sont pourris.
Aient esté seigneurs ou dames
Souef et tendrement nourris
De cresme, fromentee ou riz,
Leurs os sont declinez en pouldre
Auxquelz ne chault d'esbatz ne ris.
Plaise au doulx Jhesus les absouldre.

180

Aux trespassez je fais ce laiz
Et icelluy je communique
A regens, cours, sieges, palaiz,
Hayneurs d'avarice l'inique
Lesquelz pour la chose publique
Se seichent les os et les corps.
De Dieu et de saint Domique
Soient absols quant seront mors.

178

These heads have bowed and scraped to one
another once. Some ruled the roost,
some served in awe; all dead and done.
I see their bodies all reduced
pellmell to heaps, the lands they used
to run usurped. There is no leave
for any appeal to be produced.
Master or clerk, there's no reprieve.

179

God rest their souls now they are dead.
As for their bodies, they are dust,
lords though they were and ladies fed
tenderly, sweetly on cream and custard,
pudding and rice. Their bones are just
fined down to powder; they have no call
for laughter, no jig for joy or lust.
May sweet Jesus absolve them all.

180

For all those dead and gone I make
this legacy and make it plain
to regents, courts, tribunals that take
a stand against all greed, and drain
their bones and bodies to sustain
the common good. By God and by
St Dominic,[61] may they all gain
their absolution when they die.

181

Item: riens a Jacquet Cardon
Car je n'ay riens pour luy d'honneste –
Non pas que le gette habandon –
Sinon ceste bergeronnette;
S'elle eust le chant 'Marionnette',
Fait pour Marion la Peautarde,
Ou d' 'Ouvrez vostre huys, Guillemette'.
Elle allast bien a la moustarde:

182

CHANSON

Au retour de dure prison
Ou j'ai laissié presque la vie,
Se Fortune a sur moy envie,
Jugiez s'elle fait mesprison.
Il me semble que par raison
Elle deust bien estre assouvie
Au retour.

Se si plaine est de desraison
Que vueille que du tout devie,
Plaise a Dieu que l'ame ravie
En soit lassus en sa maison,
Au retour.

183

Item: donne a maistre Lomer
Comme extraict que je suis de fee
Qu'il soit bien amé – mais d'amer
Fille en chief ou femme coeffee
Ja n'en ayt la teste eschauffee –
Et qu'il ne luy couste une noix
Faire ung soir cent fois la faffee
En despit d'Ogier le Danois.

181

Item: for Jacques Cardon, nix.
I've nothing decent left for him
but I won't leave him in a fix.
Perhaps a song will take his whim.
The tune is 'Marionette', a hymn
to Marion the Skintight; or try
'Open your door, Guillemette', a trim
piece that might serve for mustard pie.

182

SONG

On my return from the harsh prison
where I almost lost my life,
if Fate has even now her knife
in me, you judge of her decision:
it seems to me, without derision
she now should put an end to strife,
                              on my return.

If she is mad beyond revision
and I no longer may survive,
pray God my rapt soul may arrive
within his house above when risen,
                              on my return.

183

Item: to Master Lomer I give,
since I was fairy born, the jinx
of love while he's unamative
from cover girl and hatless minx!
And may he plug a hundred chinks
a night that cost him a mere nut,
despite whatever Ogier thinks,
that great Dane with a nose for smut.

184

Item: donne aux amans enfermes –
Sans le laiz maistre Alain Chartier –
A leurs chevez, de pleurs et lermes
Trestout fin plain ung benoistier
Et ung petit brain d'esglantier
Qui soit tout vert, pour guipillon,
Pourveu qu'ilz diront ung psaultier
Pour l'ame du povre Villon.

185

Item: a maistre Jacques Jammes
Qui se tue d'amasser biens
Donne fiancer tant de femmes
Qu'il vouldra, mais d'espouser riens.
Pour qui amasse il? Pour les siens.*
Il ne plaint fors que ses morceaulx.
Ce qui fut aux truyes, je tiens
Qu'il doit de droit estre aux pourceaulx.

186

Item: le camus Seneschal†
Qui une fois paya mes debtes,
En recompence, mareschal
Sera pour ferrer oes et canettes.
Je luy envoie ces sornettes
Pour soy desennuyer. Combien,
S'il veult face en des alumettes.
De bien chanter s'ennuye on bien!

*Longnon-Foulet takes this line as two questions. I make the second a statement as a more mordant comment on the previous line which he takes as a question and negative answer. In this latter point I follow Kinnell.

†Longnon-Foulet has 'sera le' in place of 'le camus' and then opens the fourth line with 'Pour ferrer . . .' which gives a better syllable count.

184

Item: for couples who can't quite make it –
beside the Chartier[62] bequest –
an aspersorium of naked
tears, with a sprig of wild rose dressed,
beside their bed to beat their breast,
forever green to cast aspersion –
so long as they will sing to rest
poor Villon's soul with psalms in person.

185

Item: to Jacques James I wish
(he'll kill himself to make a mint)
that he may pick and choose his dish
but marry no one. The skinflint
will claim to all but kin he's skint.
His only whine is where to dine.
The filth of sows, to drop a hint,
most rightfully belongs to swine.

186

The Seneschal with the snub nose
(who once from debt bought my release)
in recompense I now propose
to make a smith to shoe the geese
and ducks.[63] I send these jokes to please
him. Never mind if he desires
to make light with them at his ease,
for in the end good singing tires.

187

Item: au Chevalier du Guet
Je donne deux beaulx petiz pages,
Philebert et le gros Marquet,
Qui tres bien servy, comme sages,*
La plus partie de leurs aages,
Ont le prevost des mareschaulx.
Helas, s'ilz sont cassez de gages,
Aller les fauldra tous deschaulx.

188

Item: a Chappelain je laisse
Ma chappelle a simple tonsure,
Chargiee d'une seiche messe
Ou il ne fault pas grant lecture.
Resigné luy eusse ma cure
Mais point ne veult de charge d'ames.
De confesser, ce dit, n'a cure
Sinon chamberieres et dames.

189

Pour ce que scet bien mon entente
Jehan de Calais, honnorable homme,
Qui ne me vit des ans a trente
Et ne scet comment je me nomme,
De tout ce testament, en somme,
S'aucun y a difficulté,
L'oster jusqu'au rez d'une pomme
Je luy en donne faculté,

*Both Bonner and Kinnell take this line as 'Lesquelz servy, dont sont plus sages'. Longnon–Foulet, which I follow, seems slightly less awkward.

187

Item: to the Captain of the Watch
I give two handsome little pages,
Filbert and Marquet, both a notch
in the Provost Marshall's belt for ages,
or most of theirs, and more like sages
for all the services they know.
If laid off now and no one engages
them then barefoot they must go.

188

Item: to Chappelain I pass
my lowly cleric's chapel. True,
there's not much reading, a dry mass,
that's all it needs. I'd give him too
my cure but that would hardly do.
He doesn't like the care of souls
and hates confession but gets through
the maids and ladies, picking holes.

189

Because he takes my meaning well,
to Jean de Calais comes this right
(though he's not seen me for a spell
of thirty years and never quite
recalls my name): if what I write
in my last will is hard to see
or difficult, let him shed light
and prune it like an apple-tree,

190

De le gloser et commenter,
De le diffinir et descripre,
Diminuer ou augmenter,
De le canceller et prescripre
De sa main, et ne sceut escripre,
Interpreter et donner sens
A son plaisir, meilleur ou pire.
A tout cecy je m'y consens.

191

Et s'aucun dont n'ay congnoissance
Estoit allé de mort a vie
Je vueil et luy donne puissance
Affin que l'ordre soit suyvie,
Pour estre mieulx parassouvie,
Que ceste aumosne ailleurs transporte
Sans se l'appliquer par envie.
A son ame je m'en rapporte.

192

Item: j'ordonne a Sainte Avoye
Et non ailleurs ma sepulture.
Et affin que chascun me voie –
Non pas en char mais en painture –
Que l'on tire mon estature
D'ancre s'il ne coustoit trop chier.
De tombel? riens; je n'en ay cure
Car il greveroit le planchier.

190

or gloss, define and annotate;
transcribe, diminish, or augment;
cancel, suppress or regulate
by his own hand with my consent;
and if he cannot tell what's meant,
to make what sense of it he can
for better or worse to his content.
In all of this I trust the man.

191

Should any here have passed from death
to life without my knowledge, I wish
the said Calais to see my breadth
of vision quite fulfilled and dish
my alms out to the pauperish.
But if he keeps them in his greed
I leave his conscience to swish
about him till he mends the deed.

192

Item: I wish to be laid to rest
in St Avoye – no other place.
And so they see me at my best
(not in the flesh; what paint can trace)
I'll have my portrait, figure and face,
life-size in ink if it's no great
expense. A tomb? No, not the space,
besides, the floor won't bear the weight.

193

Item: vueil qu'autour de ma fosse
Ce qui s'ensuit sans autre histoire
Soit escript en lettre assez grosse
Et qui n'auroit point d'escriptoire
De charbon ou de pierre noire
Sans en riens entamer le plastre.
Au moins sera de moi memoire
Telle qu'elle est d'ung bon follastre:

194

Epitaph

Cy gist et dort en ce sollier
Qu'amours occist de son raillon
Ung povre petit escollier
Qui fut nommé Françoys Villon.
Oncques de terre n'eut sillon;
Il donna tout, chascun le scet:
Tables, tresteaulx, pain, corbeillon.
Gallans, dictes en ce verset:

195

RONDEAU

Repos eternel donne a cil,
Sire, et clarté perpetuelle,
Qui vaillent plat ni escuelle
N'eut oncques, n'ung brain de percil.
Il fut rez, chief, barbe et sourcil
Comme ung navet qu'on ret ou pelle:
Repos eternel donne a cil.

193

Item: upon my grave, I think,
without embellishment, in large
letters, what follows. (If there's no ink,
carbon or coal will do my charge.)
Don't crack the plaster with a barge-
pole, take some care and let men see
the legend of me still at large,
of one who lived fool-heartily:

194

Epitaph

Here in this garret lies and sleeps
one whom love's arrows shot and killed,
a poor worthless scholar home for keeps,
named François Villon. He never tilled
a field nor ploughed his furrow. He willed
his all away: tables, beds, his bread
and baskets. Gallants with glass now filled
recite this verse for one now dead:

195

RONDEAU

Grant him eternal rest now dead,
Oh lord, and everlasting light.
He wasn't worth the candle, quite,
or even a parsley sprig. His head
was shorn, his beard and eyebrows shed –
a turnip scraped and scoured white.
Grant him eternal rest now dead.

Rigueur le transmit en exil
Et luy frappa au cul la pelle
Non obstant qu'il dit, 'J'en appelle!'
– Qui n'est pas terme trop subtil.
Repos eternel donne a cil.

196

Item: je vueil qu'on sonne a bransle
Le gros beffroy qui est de voirre
Combien qu'il n'est cuer qui ne tremble
Quant de sonner est a son erre.
Sauvé a mainte bonne terre,
Le temps passé, chascun le scet.
Fussent gens d'armes ou tonnerre,
Au son de luy tout mal cessoit.

197

Les sonneurs auront quatre miches
Et se c'est peu, demye douzaine.
Autant n'en donnent les plus riches,
Mais ilz seront de saint Estienne.
Vollant est homme de grant paine,
L'ung en sera – quant g'y regarde,
Il en vivra une sepmaine.
Et l'autre? Au fort, Jehan de la Garde.

198

Pour tout ce fournir et parfaire
J'ordonne mes executeurs
Auxquels fait bon avoir affaire
Et contentent bien leurs debteurs!
Ilz ne sont pas moult grans vanteurs
Et ont bien de quoy, Dieu mercis,
De ce fait seront directeurs.
Escry, je t'en nommerai six:

Strict justice banished him and sped
his arse up with a spade all right.
He cried: 'Appeal!' not subtle, quite.
God grant him eternal rest now dead.

196

Item: I'd like someone to peal
the great bell – the one that's made
of glass – though everyone must feel,
hearing the sound, his heart's afraid
for it has warned of storm or raid
and saved rich soil in recent times.
Whether thunder or armed men invade
all evil ceases when it chimes.

197

Four loaves the ringers shall receive
or half a dozen if four's too few,
(as much as that the rich don't leave!)
but rockcakes of St Stephen. Now who?
Volant is careful; he will do,
but come to think of it, his share
will last him for the whole week through.
The other? John the Guard is spare.

198

To accomplish and achieve so much
I'll name executors below:
such men who have the business touch
and keep their debtors happy. You know
they're not the greatest boasters, though
they have the wherewithal, thank God.
They'll take full charge on the whole show.
I'll name you six: record this squad:

199

C'est maistre Martin Bellefaye,
Lieutenant du cas criminel;
Qui sera l'autre? G'y pensoye . . .
Ce sera sire Colombel.
S'il luy plaist et il luy est bel
Il entreprendra ceste charge.
Et l'autre? Michiel Jouvenel.
Ces trois seulz et pour tout, j'en charge.

200

Mais, ou cas qu'ilz s'en excusassent
En redoubtant les premiers frais
Ou totallement recusassent,
Ceulx qui s'enssuivent cy après
Institue, gens de bien tres:
Phelip Brunel, noble escuyer;
Et l'autre? Son voisin d'emprès,
Si est maistre Jaques Raguier.

201

Et l'autre? Maistre Jaques James –
Trois hommes de bien et d'onneur,
Desirans de sauver leurs ames
Et doubtans Dieu Nostre Seigneur.
Plus tost y mecteront du leur★
Que ceste ordonnance ne baillent.
Point n'auront de contrerolleur,
Mais a leur bon plaisir en taillent.

★Kinnell reads 'mecteront' which I follow where Longnon-Foulet reads 'mettroient'. He also omits 'Mais' in the last line and reads 'bon seul plaisir'. Longnon-Foulet reads more naturally, I think.

199

Martin Bellefaye for one I name –
the Criminal Lieutenant. And two?
I've thought that out. I have a claim
on Sire Colombel, and if he knew
it would amuse him or accrue
something he would perform the task.
Third? Michel Jouvenal will do.
To take sole charge these three I'll ask.

200

But if they make some poor excuse,
fearing the outlay, or point-blank
refuse, I therefore must induce
the following: all men of rank
and breeding: Philippe Brunel, I'll thank,
a noble squire, and next his neighbour,
Jacques Raguier, on him I bank;
and lastly Master James's favour.

201

All three are good honourable men,
seeking salvation for their souls,
fearing the Lord their God. These then
would lose pocket, go in holes,
rather than not fulfil their rôles
in this my ordinance. There'll be
no other over them who controls
the way things go: they'll make quite free.

202

Des testamens qu'on dit le Maistre
De mon fait n'aura *quid* ne *quod*.
Mais ce sera ung jeune prestre
Qui est nommé Thomas Tricot.
Voulentiers beusse a son escot
Et qu'il me coustast ma cornete.
S'il sceust jouer a ung tripot
Il eust de moyle Trou Perrete.

203

Quant au regart du luminaire
Guillaume du Ru j'y commetz;
Pour porter les coings du suaire,
Aux executeurs le remetz.
Trop plus mal me font qu'onques mais
Barbe, cheveulx, penil, sourcis.
Mal me presse; temps desormais
Que crie a toutes gens mercis.

204

BALLADE

A Chartreux et a Celestins,
A Mendians et a Devotes,
A musars et claquepatins,
A servans et filles mignotes
Portans surcotz et justes cotes,
A cuidereaux d'amours transsis
Chaussans sans meshaing fauves botes,
Je crie a toutes gens mercis.

202

But not a thing for the Probate Court,
but rather for a youngster priest,
Thomas Tricot. I'll drink a short
on him although it cost at least
my yard. To him when I've deceased
will come the rights to *Perrette's Hole*;
but only when his skill's increased
at tennis. Strokeplay has its rôle!

203

Guillaume de Ru will be in charge
of all the funerary lamps.
For pall-bearers the choice is large:
my executors will choose.
                              Pain clamps
my groin, scalp, chin and brows. The cramps
come worse than they have ever done.[64]
I'm racked and pain upon me ramps –
Time to seek pardon from everyone.

204

BALLADE

To hermits, Carthusian or Celestine,
To Devotee and Friar – to heel,
servant, trim little piece and queen
who wear tunics and coats a deal
too tight; to lovesick fops who kneel
wearing their boots of yellow tan,
and never make complaint or squeal:
pardon I cry from every man.

Le Testament

A filletes monstrans tetins
Pour avoir plus largement d'hostes,
A ribleurs, mouveurs de hutins,
A bateleurs, traynans marmotes,
A folz, folles, a sotz et sotes
Qui s'en vont siflant six a six,
A marmosetz et mariotes,
Je crie a toutes gens mercis.

Sinon aux traistres chiens matins
Qui m'ont fait chier dur et crostes*
Maschier mains soirs et mains matins,
Qu'ores je ne crains pas trois crotes.
Je feisse pour eulx petz et rotes –
Je ne puis car je suis assis.
Au fort, pour eviter riotes,
Je crie a toutes gens mercis.

Qu'on leur froisse les quinze costes
De gros mailletz, fors et massis;
De plombees et telz pelotes –
Je crie a toutes gens mercis.

205

AUTRE BALLADE

Icy se clost le testament
Et finist du pauvre Villon.
Venez a son enterrement
Quant vous orrez le carillon
Vestus rouge com vermillon
Car en amours mourut martir.
Ce jura il sur son couillon
Quant de ce monde voult partir.

*Longnon–Foulet reads 'chier dures' and omits 'et'. I follow Kinnell.

To whores who let their tits be seen
to draw a larger clientele;
to brawlers, con-men on the scene,
to showmen with their apes at heel
to fools and those in farce who steal
away, whistling, six to the van;
to dolls on strings – in hand or real –
pardon I cry from every man.

Except those sons of bitches so mean
they made dry crusts my daily meal
and made me shit hard in between,
not three turds more now can I feel
though farts and belches I would peal
for them if sitting down I can.
And yet to end all rows for real:
pardon I cry from every man.

Let someone bang their ribs a deal
with good stout weighty mallets; fan
their heads with lead weights till they reel;
pardon I cry from every man!

205

ANOTHER BALLADE

Here ends at last the Testament
of poor Villon. When next you hear
the passing bell, you should lament
in loudest red behind the bier.[65]
He died of love, he made that clear
and swore it on his only ball –
disseminated love from here to here:
prepared to leave the world and all.

Et je croy bien que pas n'en ment,
Car chassié fut comme ung souillon
De ses amours hayneusement
Tant que d'icy a Roussillon
Brosse n'y a ne brossillon
Qui n'eust, ce dit il sans mentir,
Ung lambeau de son cotillon
Quant de ce monde voult partir.

Il est ainsi et tellement:
Quant mourut n'avoit qu'ung haillon;
Qui plus, en mourant, mallement
L'espoignoit d'amours l'esguillon,
Plus agu que le ranguillon
D'ung baudrier luy faisoit sentir –
C'est de quoy nous esmerveillons –
Quant de ce monde voult partir.

Prince, gent comme esmerillon,
Sachiez qu'il fist au departir.
Ung traict but de vin morillon
Quant de ce monde voult partir.

He spoke no lie, or never meant
to lie, I'm sure. It would appear
that spiteful girls of his had sent
him haring off in mad career
like a pot-stirrer till from here
to Rousillon, each bush and wall
sported a tatter of his gear:
prepared to leave the world and all.

Those are the facts of the event:
he died in rags. Further, I fear,
as he lay dying, almost spent,
love whipped him up again in sheer
pain from its buckle-tongue (and here
we register some doubt). In gall
and agony it cost him dear:
prepared to leave the world and all.

Prince, gentle as a merlin, hear
what next he did upon the pall:
he swigged his wine, dark red and clear,
prepared to leave the world and all.

Le Debat du Cuer et du Corps de Villon

Qu'est ce que j'oy?

       Ce suis je.

              Qui?

                 Ton cuer

Qui ne tient mais qu'a ung petit filet.
Force n'ay plus, substance ne liqueur,
Quant je te voy retraict ainsi seulet
Com povre chien tapy en reculet.
Pour quoy est ce? Pour ta folle plaisance.*
Que t'en chault il?

       J'en ay la desplaisance.

Laisse m'en paix.

       Pour quoy?

            J'y penserai.

Quant sera ce?

       Quant seray hors d'enfance.

Plus ne t'en dis.

       Et je m'en passeray.

Que penses tu?

       Estre homme de valeur.

Tu as trente ans. C'est l'aage d'un mullet,†
Est ce enfance?

       Nennil.

           C'est donc folleur

Qui te saisist?

       Par ou? Par le collet?

Riens ne congnois.

       Si fais.

         Quoy?

            Mouche en let:

L'ung est blanc, l'autre est noir. C'est la distance.

*Longnon-Foulet takes the first question in this line as spoken by Villon.
I follow Bonner in taking it as a rhetorical question by the heart.
†Bonner takes this sentence as an interruption by Villon.

The Debate between Villon's Heart and Body

What's that?
>> It's only me.
>>>> But who?
>>>>>> Your heart.
I'm hanging on by just a single thread.
It saps my strength and nerve, you're so apart,
withdrawn – a corner-skulking mongrel, head
on paws. And why is this? Because you've led
a merry dance, my friend.
>>>>> So what?
>>>>>>> It's me
that takes the knocks, you know.
>>>>>>> Oh let me be.
But why?
>> So I can think of a new line
to shoot.
>> How soon?
>>>>> When childhood's over, see?
No further murmur then.
>>>>> That suits me fine.

What's on your mind?
>>>>> To play a nobler part.
You're thirty now – an age when mules are dead.
You call it childhood still?
>>>>> No more, dear heart.
Madness it must be taking hold instead.
Of what? My collar, then?
>>>>> Your empty head
knows nothing.
>>> That's not quite true at all. I see
flies in the milk as plain as they can be:
one's black, one white.

Est ce donc tout?

     Que veulx tu que je tance?
Se n'est assez, je recommenceray.
Tu es perdu.

    J'y mettray resistance.
Plus ne t'en dis.

     Et je m'en passeray.

J'en ay le dueil; *toy le mal et douleur.*
Se feusses ung povre ydiot et folet
Encore eusses de t'excuser couleur.
Si n'as tu soing: tout t'est ung, bel ou let.
Ou la teste as plus dure qu'ung jalet,
Ou mieulx te plaist qu'onneur ceste meschance.
Que respondras a ceste consequence?
J'en seray hors quant je trespasseray.
Dieu, quel confort.

     Quelle sage eloquence.
Plus ne t'en dis.

    Et je m'en passeray.

Dont vient ce mal?

     Il vient de mon maleur.
Quant Saturne me feist mon fardelet
Ces maulx y meist, je le croy.

      C'est foleur.
Son seigneur es et te tiens son varlet!
Voy que Salmon escript en son rolet,
'Homme sage,' ce dit il, 'a puissance
Sur planetes et sur leur influence.'
Je n'en croy riens; tel qu'ilz m'ont fait seray.
Que dis tu?

    Dea, certes, c'est ma creance.
Plus ne t'en dis.

    Et je m'en passeray.

                    Is that so, that the sign?
You want more argument?
                              You're lost.
                                        Not me!
No further murmur then.
                    That suits me fine.

Mine the heartache, yours, the sorrow and smart.
If you had been some simple knucklehead
then I could sometimes take your silly part,
but fair or foul's all one, I would have said,
for all you care. You have a skull of bed-
rock or you choose the life of misery
rather than honour. Now answer that for me.
Once I am dead it's no concern of mine.
Some comfort that!
                    What noble oratory!
No further murmur then.
                    That suits me fine.

Where's the trouble?
                    Bad luck from the start.
When Saturn packed my bags for me he fed
the troubles in.
                    You're mad. You take the part
of serving man when you are lord instead.
Solomon writing in his scroll has said:
'A wise man has,' it goes, 'authority
over the planets' influence.'
                              Not so with me.
I'm as they made me. That's no creed of mine.
What's that you say?
                    That's my philosophy.
No further murmur then.
                    That suits me fine.

Le Debat

Veulx tu vivre?

                  Dieu m'en doint la puissance !

Il te fault . . .

              Quoy?

                     Remors de conscience,

Lire sans fin –

              En quoy?

                      Lire en science,

Laisser les folz.

              Bien j'y adviseray.

Or le retien.

              J'en ay bien souvenance.

N'atens pas tant que tourne a desplaisance !
Plus ne t'en dis.

              Et je m'en passeray.

Very life you want?
                    God strengthen me.
It takes . . .
          Well, what?
                         Repentance it must be,
Limitless reading.
               Of what?
                              Philosophy.
Leaving all fools.
               I'll see how I incline.
Okay, remember now.
                    My memory
Never fails.
          Don't wait till worse, you see?
No further murmur then.
                    That suits me fine.

Epistre

Aiez pitié, aiez pitié de moy,
A tout le moins, si vous plaist, mes amis.
En fosse gis, non pas soubz houx ne may,
En cest exil ouquel je suis transmis
Par Fortune, comme Dieu l'a permis.
Filles, amans, jeunes gens et nouveaulx,
Danceurs, saulteurs faisans les piez de veaux,
Vifz comme dars, agus comme aguillon,
Gousiers tintans cler comme cascaveaux,
Le lesserez la, le povre Villon?

Chantres chantans a plaisance sans loy,
Galans rians, plaisans en fais et dis,
Courens, alans, francs de faulx or, d'aloy,
Gens d'esperit – ung petit estourdis –
Trop demourez car il meurt entandis.
Faiseurs de laiz, de motetz et rondeaux,
Quant mort sera vous lui ferez chaudeaux.
Ou gist, il n'entre escler ne tourbillon.
De murs espoix on lui a fait bandeaux.
Le lesserez la, le povre Villon?

Venez le veoir en ce piteux arroy,
Nobles hommes, francs de quart et de dix,
Qui ne tenez d'empereur ne de roy
Mais seulement de Dieu de Paradis.
Jeuner lui fault dimenches et merdis,
Dont les dens a plus longues que ratteaux.
Après pain sec, non pas après gasteaux,
En ses boyaulx verse eaue a gros bouillon.
Bas en terre, table n'a ne tresteaulx.
Le lesserez la, le povre Villon?

Ballade: Epistle[1]

Have a care, take care of me!
my friends, at least, my friends – please.
I'm ditched, no holly hedge or tree
for shelter. Fate for once agrees
with God to exile me. I'll freeze.
My girls, you lovers, greenhorns, gay
dancers and pairs in the Antic Hey,
prickers of spurs and darts in air,
titters that ring like bells on a sleigh:
poor Villon, will you leave him there?

Singers of songs whose tongues make free,
dandies in words and deeds that please,
you bums without a franc or fee,
you wits so absent-minded – seize
the chance – he dies by slow degrees.
Makers of motet, sonnet, lay,
your wedding breakfasts won't convey
much warmth where winds nor lightnings dare:
thick walls blindfold his eyes from day:
poor Villon, will you leave him there?

His state you ought to come and see,
nobles that own no fealties
to lord or king unless it be
to God. On Sundays, Tuesdays, he's
to fast as well: bread without cheese
washed down the water treatment way.
His teeth like a rake's rot and decay.
He lies on earth that's dank and bare,
no bed nor chair for him today:
poor Villon, will you leave him there?

Epistre

Princes nommez, ancïens, jouvenceaux,
Impetrez moy graces et royaulx seaux
Et me montez en quelque corbillon;
Ainsi le font, l'un a l'autre, pourceaux
Car ou l'un brait, ilz fuyent a monceaux.
Le lesserez la, le povre Villon?

Princes here named, the young or grey,
the king's pardon you could sway
to raise him back into the air
inside a basket. Pigs, they say,
will do as much for swine that stray:
poor Villon, will you leave him there?

Requeste a Monseigneur de Bourbon

Le mien seigneur et prince redoubté,
Fleuron de lys, royalle geniture,
Françoys Villon que Travail a dompté
A coups orbes par force de bature,
Vous supplie par ceste humble escripture
Que lui faciez quelque gracieux prest.
De s'obliger en toutes cours est prest
Si ne doubtez que bien ne vous contente :
Sans y avoir dommaige n'interest
Vous n'y perdrez seulement que l'attente.

A prince n'a ung denier emprunté
Fors a vous seul, vostre humble creature.
De six escus que luy avez presté
Cela pieça il meist en nourriture.
Tout se paiera ensemble – c'est droiture –
Mais ce sera legierement et prest.
Car se du glan rencontre en la forest
D'entour Patay et chastaignes ont vente
Paié serez sans delay ny arrest.
Vous n'y perdrez seulement que l'attente.

Si je peusse vendre de ma santé
A ung Lombart, usurier par nature,
Faulte d'argent m'a si fort enchanté
Que j'en prendroie, ce cuide, l'adventure.
Argent ne pens a gippon n'a sainture.
Beau sire Dieux, je m'esbaïs que c'est
Que devant moy croix ne se comparoist
Si non de bois ou pierre, que ne mente.

Request to Mgr de Bourbon

My Lord and prince of high renown,
the flower of the royal line,
François Villon, whom dull blows down
repeatedly by force or fine,
implores you by letter to assign
a gracious loan to him for now.
In any court he's game to vow,
so never doubt he won't repay
interest-free, intact somehow.
All you will waste is the delay.

From no prince he's borrowed a brown
penny but you; remains, in fine,
your humble servant. The odd crown
you've lent he's long since spent on wine
and food. He'll pay you, in the line
of justice, both at once; and how
lightly and swiftly you'll allow.
He'll head for acorns near Patay
to sell as nuts; no stalling now!
All you will waste is the delay.

If some born Lombard bought cash-down,
I'd almost sell some health of mine,
so desperate am I for a crown
or two. No money belts confine
my waist. Good God, I've seen no sign
of fivers over which I'd bow,
unless you count stigmata now
in stone or wood. But, truth to say,
should the true cross-piece shine, I vow
all you will waste is the delay.

Mais s'une fois la vraye m'apparoist
Vous n'y perdrez seulement que l'attente.

Prince du lys qui a tout bien complaist,
Que cuidez vous comment il me desplaist
Quant je ne puis venir a mon entente?
Bien m'entendez: aidez moy, s'il vous plaist.
Vous n'y perdrez seulement que l'attente.

Au dos de la lettre

Allez, lettres, faictes ung sault –
Combien que n'ayez pié ne langue –
Remonstrez en vostre harangue
Que faulte d'argent si m'assault.

O Prince whom all the goods endow,
consider my annoyance now
my wishes fail for lack of pay;
you understand me, help somehow.
All you will waste is the delay.

On the Back of the Letter

Go, letter, and make a splash.
Though lacking foot and mouth, yet weep
and show without appearing cheap
I'm pestered by a lack of cash.

Quatrain

Je suis Françoys dont il me poise,
Né de Paris emprès Pontoise;
Et de la corde d'une toise
Sçaura mon col que mon cul poise.

Quatrain[2]

Francis I am, which weighs me down
born in Paris near Pontoise town,
and with a stretch of rope my pate
will learn for once my arse's weight.

L'Epitaphe Villon

Freres humains qui après nous vivez
N'ayez les cuers contre nous endurcis
Car se pitié de nous povres avez
Dieu en aura plus tost de vous mercis.
Vous nous voiez cy attachez cinq, six.
Quant de la chair que trop avons nourrie,
Elle est pieça devorée et pourrie,
Et nous, les os, devenons cendre et pouldre.
De nostre mal personne ne s'en rie
Mais priez Dieu que tous nous vueille absouldre.

Se freres vous clamons, pas n'en devez
Avoir desdaing, quoy que fusmes occis
Par justice. Toutesfois, vous sçavez
Que tous hommes n'ont pas bon sens rassis.
Excusez nous, puis que sommes transsis,
Envers le fils de la Vierge Marie
Que sa grace ne soit pour nous tarie
Nous preservant de l'infernale fouldre.
Nous sommes mors; ame ne nous harie
Mais priez Dieu que tous nous vueille absouldre.

La pluye nous a debuez et lavez
Et le soleil dessechiez et noircis.
Pies, corbeaulx, nous ont les yeux cavez
Et arrachié la barbe et les sourcis.
Jamais nul temps nous ne sommes assis;
Puis ça, puis la, comme le vent varie
A son plaisir sans cesser nous charie,
Plus becquetez d'oiseaulx que dez a couldre.
Ne soiez donc de nostre confrairie
Mais priez Dieu que tous nous vueille absouldre.

Villon's Epitaph[3]

Brothers that live when we are dead,
don't set yourselves against us too.
If you could pity us instead,
then God may sooner pity you.
We five or six strung up to view,
dangling the flesh we fed so well,
are eaten piecemeal, rot and smell.
We bones in a fine dust shall fall.
No one make that a laugh to tell:
pray God may save us one and all.

Brothers, if that's the word we said,
it's no disparagement to you
although in justice we hang dead.
Yet all the same you know how few
are men of sense in all they do.
Pray now we're dead that Jesu's well
of grace shall not run dry – nor Hell
open in thunder as we fall.
We're dead; don't harry us as well:
pray God may save us one and all.

Showered and rinsed with rain, we dead
the sun has dried out black and blue.
Magpie and crow gouge out each head
for eyes and pluck the hairs. On view,
never at rest a moment or two,
winds blow us here or there a spell;
more pricked than a tailor's thumb could tell
we're needled by the birds. Don't fall
then for our brotherhood and cell:
pray God may save us one and all.

L'Epitaphe Villon

Prince Jhesus qui sur tous a maistrie
Garde qu'Enfer n'ait de nous seigneurie.
A luy n'ayons que faire ne que souldre.
Hommes, icy n'a point de mocquerie ;
Mais priez Dieu que tous nous vueille absouldre.

Prince, Lord of Men, oh keep us well
beyond the sovereignty of Hell.
On him we've no business to call.
And, men, it's no joke now I tell:
pray God may save us one and all.

Louenge a la Court de Parlement

Tous mes cinq sens: yeulx, oreilles et bouche,
Le nez, et vous, le sensitif aussi –
Tous mes membres ou il y a reprouche,
En son endroit ung chascun die ainsi:
'Souvraine Court par qui sommes icy,
Vous nous avez gardé de desconfire.
Or la langue seule ne peut souffire
A vous rendre souffissantes louenges.
Si parlons tous, fille du souvrain Sire,
Mere des bons et seur des benois anges.'

Cuer, fendez vous ou percez d'une broche,
Et ne soyez au moins plus endurcy
Qu'au desert fut la forte bise roche
Dont le peuple de Juifs fut adoulcy.
Fondez lermes et venez a mercy.
Comme humble cuer qui tendrement souspire
Louez la Court, conjointe au Saint Empire,
L'eur des Françoys, le confort des estranges,
Procreee lassus ou ciel empire,
Mere des bons et seur des benois anges.

Et vous, mes dens – chascune si s'esloche –
Saillez avant, rendez toutes mercy
Plus hautement qu'orgue, trompe, ne cloche,
Et de maschier n'ayez ores soussy.
Considerez que je feusse transsy,
Foye, pommon et rate, qui respire.
Et vous, mon corps – qui vil estes et pire
Qu'ours, ne porceau qui fait son nyt es fanges –
Louez la Court avant qu'il vous empire,
Mere des bons et seur des benois anges.

Homage to the Court[4]

[Written after Parliament had commuted his death-
sentence to banishment from Paris.]

All of my five senses, eyes, mouth, ears, nose,
and you, old sensitive, lend your support.
All of my parts now in reproach propose,
each in its proper place, these words: 'O Court,
by whose good offices we weren't cut short,
you've saved us all from death. With one accord –
since tongue alone can't of itself afford
sufficient praise – we'll speak up as we should
together, daughter of our Sovereign Lord,
sister of angels, mother of those who're good.'

Break, heart, or be run through, but don't suppose
at least you're any harder than the sort
of hard grey rock that, struck by Moses, flows
with water for the Jews. Weep tears, in short,
tenderly sighing, humble in heart and thought.
Extol the Court, defence of all abroad,
the joy of France, created by the Lord
in heaven's kingdom, and, by neighbourhood,
joined with the Holy Empire in accord,
sister of angels, mother of those who're good.

And you, my teeth, all loose enough, God knows,
leap out and give the Court a good report,
louder than trumpet, bell or organ goes.
And as for chewing, never give it a thought.
Lights, lungs, and guts that still with me consort,
just think: I might be dead. You're not ignored,
body, more foul than swine whose bed and board
is shit. Before you mess up more you should
allow the Court all praise you can afford,
sister of angels, mother of those who're good.

Louenge a la Court de Parlement

Prince, trois jours ne vueillez m'escondire
Pour moy pourveoir et aux miens 'a Dieu' dire.
Sans eulx argent je n'ay, icy n'aux changes.
Court triumphant, *fiat*, sans me desdire,
Mere des bonnes et seur des benois anges.

Prince, would you spare me three more days to sort
my things out and to say good-bye? I'm short
of cash unless I see my folks. (I'm stood
off by the changers.) *Fiat*, triumphant Court,
sister of angels, mother of those who're good.

Question au Clerc du Guichet

Que vous semble de mon appel,
Garnier? Feis je sens ou folie?
Toute beste garde sa pel.
Qui la contraint, efforce ou lie,
S'elle peult elle se deslie.
Quant donc par plaisir voluntaire
Chantee me fut ceste omelie
Estoit il lors temps de moy taire?

Se feusse des hoirs Hue Cappel
Qui fut extrait de boucherie
On ne m'eust parmy ce drappel
Faire boire en ceste escorcherie.
Vous entendez bien joncherie?
Mais quant ceste paine arbitraire
On me jugea par tricherie
Estoit il lors temps de moy taire?

Cuidiez vous que soubz mon cappel
N'y eust tant de philosophie*
Comme de dire: 'J'en appel'?
Si avoit, je vous certiffie,
Combien que point trop ne m'y fie.
Quant on me dist, present notaire,
'Pendu serez!' je vous affie,
Estoit il lors temps de moy taire?

Prince, se j'eusse eu la pepie
Pieça je feusse ou est Clotaire
Aux champs debout comme une espie;
Estoit il lors temps de moy taire?

*I follow Longnon-Foulet here. Other texts read 'N'ëust . . .' which is
rare and extraordinary.

Question to the Clerk at the Gate[5]

What do you think of my appeal,
Garnier? Was it right or wrong?
Every creature gives a squeal
before it's hurt and makes a song
and dance to save its skin. How long
then, when they lectured me to death
for their amusement, should I, strong
and silent, hold my bated breath?

I would have had a better deal
as heir of Hue Cappel (a long
line of butchers). Then, I feel,
no drop could ever touch my tongue
through cloth. You see? Don't get me wrong.
But when they sentenced me to death
and pulled a fast one, should I, strong
and silent, hold my bated breath?

Under my hat, you thought, the real
grey matter hardly could belong
to tell them all that I appeal.
There was, I promise you, headstrong
enough never to trust that throng.
So when they sentenced me to death
by hanging, should I have gone along
and, silent, hold my bated breath?

Prince, if I had lost my song
I'd be where Clotaire lies in death
or like a lookout, the drop long,
and, silent, hold my bated breath.

Notes

I have not attempted in these notes to explain every allusion. With Villon, this would be an impossibly cumbersome task and a scholar's life work. This edition is intended as a reading one rather than an academic. I have therefore concentrated on cross-referencing the characters who appear in both the main works and noting the major decisions taken in translation. The stanzas are numbered for ease of reference, and for this purpose, ballades and rondeaux etc., are treated as one stanza or poem. Many stanzas in Villon are still open to interpretation and the reader can make his guess without being nudged by notes. A rule of thumb would be that if there is the ghost of a pun or an innuendo it was intended! A general point that may be made here is that the italicized names, such as *Le Hëaulme*, are not pub-signs but house-signs used in Paris at this period.

LE LAIS

Stanza 1 Note 1   I am virtually convinced that the inconclusive syntax of this stanza is a joking reflection upon 'mind and senses clear'. The opening line of the next stanza reinforces this view. Vegetius was a fourth-century Roman, author of *De Re Militari*.

Stanza 2 Note 2   As Pound has said Villon always rhymes on the definite word. Not much you can do about it in English, hence these assonances instead of full rhyme.

Stanza 4 Note 3   The allusion in the last line to ploughing is as much sexual as agricultural. I omit a similar innuendo concerning 'coining' for reasons of space and versification.

Stanza 6 Note 4   It seems to have been criminal investigations over the robbery of the College of Navarre as much as love that made Villon leave Paris in haste.

Stanza 10 Note 5   You cannot always put a foreign author's puns in the right place. This is a poor attempt to catch the flavour of several missing ones.

Stanza 11 *Note* 6   Ythier Marchant: a boyhood friend of Villon's, born of a wealthy family. He became important in Burgundian politics until bought off by Louis XI who hated him. Later he was involved in a plot to poison the king and finished up in the dungeons where he died in 1474. The sword Villon gives is a 'branc' which may pun on 'bran' meaning 'excrement'.

Le Cornu was rich and worked in state finance and then as criminal clerk in the Châtelet. He died in 1476 of the plague.

Stanza 12 *Note* 7   Saint Amant Villon hated. As clerk of the Treasury he had great influence. He seems to have been of poor mettle, sexless and dull. (See *Le Testament*, stanza 105)

Stanza 12 *Note* 8   Blarru was a goldsmith. The gift of a zebra is a puzzle – though I should think from its antics it had a sexual significance.

Stanza 12 *Note* 9   This refers to a papal decree of 1215 ordering all christians to confess with their parish priest once a year. Villon restores the decree for them out of his hatred for the Mendicants who had rights of hearing confession granted in 1449.

Stanza 13 *Note* 10   Robert Vallée: son of a family of rich financiers, he seems from this stupid and hen-pecked.

Stanza 16 *Note* 11   Jacques Cardon: a rich clothier in no need of gloves and capes.

Stanza 17 *Note* 12   Regnier de Montigny: born of an important family that had come down in the world, he turned early to crime and probably was the man who introduced Villon to the underworld. He was hanged in Paris in 1457.

For Jean Raguier the only further information is in *Le Testament*, stanza 113.

Stanza 18 *Note* 13   The Seigneur de Grigny, Philippe Brunel, was a truculent noble who tried to mend his fortune by robbing his own church, for which he spent fourteen months in prison and set the law-court against him by his truculence in reply. The buildings bequeathed to him were ruins in Villon's time.

Stanza 19 *Note* 14   Jacques Raguier: possibly son of Charles VII's master cook – also from this a master drunk. There is a suggestion too that he was a master lecher – which I have hinted at in the pun on 'share' and 'plough-share' (see note 3).

Stanza 20 Note 15 Jean Mautaint was Examiner at the Châtelet. He investigated the robbery of the College of Navarre.

Pierre Basanier: notary at the Châtelet.

Their lord was the Provost Robert d'Estouteville who seems to have taken an interest in Villon's case. As head of the police he was extremely powerful (see *Le Testament*, stanza 147–8.)

Stanza 20 Note 16 The lawyer is named in the French as Pierre Fournier; something had to give in the versification! He was not in fact Villon's lawyer but lawyer to the community of Saint-Benoît at the Châtelet.

Stanza 21 Note 17 Jean Trouvé was an assistant butcher; the gifts he is offered, though appropriate to his trade, suggest to me that he was not much use with women.

Stanza 22 Note 18 This particular Captain had his right to the post – dependent on one's nobility – challenged by someone who claimed his knighthood. Villon settles the question by giving him a mock knighthood.

'The Lily Pad' is as near as I can get to the pun in the original upon 'lis' and 'lit'. Beds would be welcome enough in prison (see *Epistre*).

Stanza 23 Note 19 Perrenet Marchant: constable and bailiff at the Châtelet none too keen on law and order. The charge here is that he is also a whoremonger. Bales of straw were strewn in prostitutes' rooms as well as in dungeons.

Stanza 24 Note 20 Jean de Loup and Casin Cholet were crooked friends of Villon's. In 1456 they were employed, God knows how, as river guards on the Seine. They presumably took advantage of this for poaching and filching as described. Wood and charcoal were easy for them to come by from the ships and boats whose loads they were meant to guard.

Stanza 25–6 Note 21 These men were old usurers of great wealth based mainly in salt supplies. 'Blanc' was a small silver coin; four would be worth about eight shillings or forty new pence. The 'delicate tasters' tries to capture the ambiguity of the French, meaning 'worms' as well as 'tit-bits'.

Stanzas 27–9 Note 22 A similar sarcasm continues here. These two are both wealthy and old and influential. It is difficult not to see a suggestion of homosexuality here and a dildo in the crozier or cue – though either would undoubtedly like to have been bishop. Letters of nomination signified a graduate's fitness for a benefice and were, of course, untransferable.

Stanza 30 *Note* 23   Windows were valuable in those days and often bequeathed. Villon had none, but presumably the spider's web is of a similar pattern.

Stanza 33 *Note* 24   Jean de la Garde was a seller of spice. There is a sexual suggestion in the imagery of mortar and pestle, especially as several spices were thought to be aphrodisiac (see *Le Testament*, stanza 119; 181). St Antony's Fire is now known as gangrenous erisipelas. For whom it was intended here is not known.

Stanza 34 *Note* 25   Pierre Merbeuf: a rich clothier.

Nicolas Louvieux: a rich magistrate and tax-collector. The Prince of Fools: a sort of Festival figure who distributed cardboard coins along the streets in imitation of the King during processions.

Stanza 35 *Note* 26   The Bell was called Marie and could be heard all over Paris on a calm day. Villon's room was only about a hundred yards away from it. It rang curfew and angelus, mentioned here.

Stanzas 36–8 *Note* 27   These stanzas mock Scholastic terms and philosophy. As for rhyming, I have left them much as they are.

Stanza 38 *Note* 28   The poem ends with a suggestion of self-love and masturbation as a direct contrast to the falseness and failure of courtly love with which the poem opens.

Stanza 40 *Note* 29   I have telescoped two implications here. 'To eat no figs or dates' may be the literal meaning; it may also mean 'Who doesn't eat, shit or piss'.

LE TESTAMENT

Stanza 1 *Note* 1   Thibault d'Aussigny: Bishop of Orleans. He had Villon locked in the dungeons for some misdemeanour.

'Blessing streets' refers to the blessing of the people lining the route of street processions.

Stanza 2 Note 2   There is a pun here on *serf* and *cerf* – difficult to render.

Stanza 5 Note 3   The Picards were an heretical sect which did not believe in prayer.

Stanza 6 Note 4   The *Deus Laudem*, seventh verse: 'Let his days be few and let another take his bishopric.' The Authorised Version differs from this translation.

Stanza 7 Note 5   King Louis XI who acceded in 1461. It was customary for prisoners to be released when the king made a progress through a town. Hence Villon's release from the dungeons of d'Aussigny's palace – and hence the rather over-done gratitude.

Stanza 9 Note 6   St Martial: a bishop of Limoges; popular etymology had confused the issue by awarding him military virtues.

Stanza 13 Note 7   The town is Moulins, residence of the Duke of Bourbon. *Esperance*, device of the Bourbons, is here translated as *hope*. Other commentators identify the town symbolically as the City of God.

Stanza 15 Note 8   *Le Roman de la Rose*: an extremely popular, long, allegorical poem of the late thirteenth and early fourteenth century, begun by Guillaume de Lorris and finished by Jean de Meung. Chaucer also draws upon it. The quotation is apparently from a prefatory poem *Le Testament* which Villon may have seen affixed to the manuscript.

Stanza 27 Note 9   'Rejoice . . .' Ecclesiastes 11:9
              'Childhood . . .' Ecclesiastes 11:10

Stanza 28 Note 10   'My days . . .' Job 7:6

Stanza 30 Note 11   Celestines and Carthusians are religious orders with a preference for the hermitical life. The reference to oyster-fishing is probably sexual but also comments on their rather unmonkish habits of dress and display.

Stanza 34 Note 12   This colloquial saying for changing the topic is literal here.

Stanza 36 Note 13   Jacques Coeur, one of the richest men in France, a financier who aided the French Government in the last days of the Hundred Years' War. He died in November 1456.

Stanza 42 Note 14   Flora: A famous Roman courtesan.

Archipiades: a blunder for Alcibiades who was in any case a man renowned for his beauty in the Middle Ages. Presumably Villon nodded off during some lecture and misheard it.

Thais: an Athenian courtesan who followed Alexander into Egypt.

Buridan: a famous fourteenth-century professor at the University of Paris, hero of a popular legend. The Queen of France and Navarre was supposed to invite students to her rooms overlooking the Seine, eat, dance and make love with them and then have them thrown into the Seine to die quietly. Buridan, disguised as a student, is supposed to have infiltrated her rooms in this way and, on being thrown into the Seine, he landed in a barge of hay prearranged to be there.

Blanche: Blanche de Castille, mother of Louis IX.

Bertha, Beatrice and Alice: heroines of *Henri de Metz*, a *chanson de geste*; the first wife of Pepin le bref, and mother of Charlemagne.

Arembourg: heir to Maine and wife of Foulques d'Anjou, she died in 1126.

Stanza 43 Note 15   Callixtus III: pope from 1455 to 1458, Alfonso de Borgia, famous for preaching a crusade against the Turks.

Alfonso V: King of Aragon and Naples, a great warrior and patron of the arts. He died in 1458.

Charles, Duke of Bourbon, died in 1456.

Arthur III, Duke of Britanny and Constable of France, died in 1458.

Charles VII: King of France from 1422 to 1461.

James II: King of Scotland, killed in 1460, besieging Roxburgh Castle.

The King of Cyprus was Jean III de Lusignan. He died in 1458.

Ladislaus, King of Bohemia, died in 1457.

Du Guesclin, constable of France under Charles V, a hero in the Hundred Years' War, died in 1380.

The Dauphin d'Auvergne may be Beraud III who died in 1426. The Duke of Alençon 'lately slain' is by a nasty joke Jean II who was not dead but deprived of his lands and titles for treason. Possibly Jean I is intended; in which case he died at the battle of Agincourt.

The whole ballade is extremely ironic since all those mentioned, except in the envoi, died between the writing of *Le Lais* in 1456 and *Le Testament* in 1461.

Stanza 44 Note 16 This ballade was written in what Villon thought was old French. I have here and there suggested this by use of archaic English poetic diction.

Stanza 50 Note 17 The Lovely Armouress was an actual whore whom Villon knew in her extreme old age before 1456. She had been favoured in youth by the powerful Nicolas d'Orgemont, son of Pierre d'Orgemont, the famous chancellor to Charles V. Nicolas d'Orgemont was a Canon of Notre-Dame and had her installed in one of the houses of the cloister. He was finally jailed for plotting against the King and died, oddly enough, in the dungeons of the Bishop of Meung.

The nickname derives from the fact that an attempt to clear the streets of prostitutes had forced the girls to double as shopkeepers. Their nicknames thus derive from their trade-cover.

When Robert Lowell made a version of this famous lament he remarked, 'I have dropped lines, moved lines, moved stanzas, changed images and altered metre and intent.' And here are the only places in this translation where I have consciously altered images to fall in with modern taste. I have done this to preserve stanzas which Lowell cut – the catalogues of sexual attributes in youth and age – in order to give them greater variety and a more concrete impact. An obvious example is 57 where 'grapeskin' is not out of Villon; in stanza 58 I have done something to tone down the repetitiousness.

Stanza 58 Note 18 This is the verse Pound alludes to in his *ABC of Reading* where he says Villon always rhymes on the definite word.

Stanza 60 Note 19 This ballade makes use of the nicknames of prostitutes derived from their shop-keeping. I have tried to anglicize them and indicate their suggestiveness at the same time. *Le Testament* makes clear the imagery as you read on.

Stanza 61 *Note* 20   Fremin: most commentators agree that this scribe is a fictitious device.

Stanza 69 *Note* 21   It is virtually impossible to translate a double ballade into English at the same time as you maintain the rhyme-scheme. I have resorted to final assonance for most of the rhymes but the translation is still far from satisfactory in that the historic present has had to be used. It is chiefly interesting for the autobiographical detail. Much of the other detail is inaccurate, obscure, or the result of a buffooning sense of humour.

Stanza 69 *Note* 22   It is interesting to note that in the penultimate stanza Villon himself seems to have strayed from the rhyme-scheme. It seems to have been a custom for wedding guests to pummel each other playfully, saying 'Remember this wedding!'

Stanza 78 *Note* 23   Tacque Thibaud was a favourite of the Duc de Berry, hated for his oppression and debauchery, but the name is clearly used here as an insulting nickname for the Bishop of Orleans, d'Aussigny.

Stanza 78 *Note* 24   'Chokepears' were (i) a fruit, (ii) a metaphor for bitterness, (iii) a torture device of metal, pear-shaped, which could be expanded by a screw after insertion in the victim's mouth. The reference to water combines the idea of bread and water and the water torture.

Stanza 79   *Note* 25   His lieutenant was Pierre Bourgoing.
His official was Etienne Plaisance, hence the pun. Robert was most likely the executioner of Orleans.

Stanza 82 *Note* 26   Moreau was a seller of roast meats; Provins was a pastry cook, and Robin Turgis owner of *Pine Cone Inn* – all three the type to whom Villon would owe debts and thus his heirs!

Stanza 93 *Note* 27   *Le Rommant du Pet au Deable*, probably about a student escapade with the house-signs of Paris, is an early work of Villon's now lost. Guy Tabary was a member of the gang that raided the College of Navarre. He is 'honest' because his blabbing let the cat out of the bag about the robbery.

Stanza 95 *Note* 28   Theophilus: hero of a legend popular then of a man who sold his soul to the Devil in order to keep his job; a version of it appears in *Le Miracle de Theophile* by Rutebeuf.

Stanza 96 *Note* 29 'Rose' refers by metaphor to Villon's girl-friend. In the ballade, verse 100, she is named acrostically as 'Marthe'.

Stanza 100 *Note* 30 The second verse of the ballade names 'Marthe' acrostically. Presumably 'Françoys' was false and 'Marthe' might have been true!

Stanza 101 *Note* 31 For Ythier Marchant, see Notes to *Le Lais*, stanza 11.

Stanza 103 *Note* 32 For Jean Le Cornu, see Notes to *Le Lais*, stanza 11.

Stanza 105 *Note* 33 For Pierre St Amant, see Notes to *Le Lais*, stanza 12.

Stanza 106 *Note* 34 Sire Dennis Hesselin was a fiscal judge.

Stanza 108 *Note* 35 Pierre Fournier was not Villon's personal lawyer but attorney to the community of Saint-Benoît at the Châtelet.

Stanza 109 *Note* 36 For Jacques Raguier, see Notes to *Le Lais*, stanza 19. Villon offers him four 'placques' in the original; they were Belgian coins of little worth. Taking a tip from *Le Lais*, I have freely translated them into the Elizabethan 'plackets'!

Stanza 110 *Note* 37 See Note to *Le Lais*, stanza 34, for these two.

Stanza 112 *Note* 38 This is a buffooning stanza throughout. He virtually gives the address of the two women. I have indicated this southern dialect by some English 'stage' dialect.

Stanza 113 *Note* 39 A cheese soufflé was slang for a punch in the face. I have used 'Côte de Maubué' to make the joke clear: Maubué was a well-known water fountain near Bailly's.

Stanza 114 *Note* 40 Michault de Four: a tipstaff of the Châtelet, he took part in the inquiry into the College of Navarre robbery.

Stanza 115 *Note* 41 The Two Hundred and Twenty were virtu-ally city police under the charge of the Provost. Villon gives the two of them a *cornete*, which means both a silk or velvet band for the hat or the hangman's hemp noose. I have tried to convey the idea with 'chinstrap' and the English idiom.

Stanza 116 *Note* 42 For Perrenet Marchant, see Notes to *Le Lais*, stanza 23.

Stanzas 117–8 *Note* 43   For Wolf and Cholet, see Notes to *Le Lais*, stanza 24.

Stanza 119 *Note* 44   The Woodsmith was probably another tip-staff. Ginger was regarded as an aphrodisiac.

Stanza 120 *Note* 45   John Riou was a furrier, chosen captain of the Hundred Archers which were a volunteer militia.

Stanza 122 *Note* 46   Robert Trascaille: clerk to Jean le Picart, treasury counsellor to the King, later a tax collector, who had no shortage of gold, let alone bowls.

Stanza 123 *Note* 47   The abbess was Huguette du Hamel, more likely to initiate her novices into sex than religion. After strong disapproval from the church, she invested the abbey's money and absconded with her lover Master Baudes le Maitre with all the titles of the abbey.

Stanza 128 *Note* 48   The original 'caige vert', probably refers to a house-sign, but the 'cage' had an erotic meaning also which I suggest as well as I can in the pun 'bird'.

Stanza 131 *Note* 49   The gorget is slang for hangman's noose. There's not much that can be done about it in English. The stanza, as a whole, with its technical vocabulary, can't be done decently into verse.

Stanza 135 *Note* 50   Here, as in most places, the coinage is used for sexual suggestion. Punning throughout, I've tried to equal the suggestiveness in English.

Stanza 137 *Note* 51   'Ave salus, tibi decus' is part of a Latin hymn to Our Lady. But *saluts* and *écus* were coins. I indicate the puns by spelling. The *Donatus* also suggests 'giving'.

Stanza 138 *Note* 52   The Great Credo was a joke for long term credit which of course these money-lenders hated. See notes to *Le Lais*, stanza 25. 'Flans', here translated '*mint*', meant both 'custards' and the 'blanks' used in coining. This was as near as I could get.

Stanza 144 *Note* 53   The riding boots are a reference to sexual intercourse. For 'Michault' see *Le Testament*, stanza 97.

Stanza 146 *Note* 54   Thibaud was a name for a cuckold. I use an Elizabethan anachronism to suggest this.

Stanza 148 *Note* 55   The ballade has Estouteville's wife's names acrostically. It should be read as coming from him – or as a Villonous joke! Estouteville apparently did all that was said of him in the previous stanza. See notes to *Le Lais*, stanza 20; note 15.

Stanza 152 *Note* 56   This ballade is the most tedious piece of Villon. It is translated here for completeness but with every evidence of impatience as the rhymes show!

Stanza 153 *Note* 57   Franc Gontier was the hero of a popular poem praising the simple life. Villon who had suffered it of necessity had no time for such naivety.

Stanza 156 *Note* 58   My Lady obviously kept a brothel. In fact, its sign *Le Pet au Diable* (The Devil's Fart) was the subject of Villon's earlier, lost poem (see *Le Testament*, stanza 93). The graveyards were likely to be the cemetery des Innocents described in stanzas 176–9, a popular place for prostitutes. The harridans of the Linen Market would give as much as they got as the following ballade suggests, one difficult to translate as it rhymes throughout on proper names more systematic than those of English.

Stanza 170 *Note* 59   Colin de Cayeux was implicated in the College of Navarre robbery with Villon. He escaped jurisdiction several times by benefit of clergy but was caught in Senlis and condemned by a secular court and hanged on 26 September 1460.

Montpipeau and Rueil were slang terms for robbing and stealing.

Stanza 175 *Note* 60   These were the patients in a hospital for the blind. They had the right to beg on holidays in the cemetery des Innocents. They will need to tell good skulls from bad, and, possibly, good prostitutes from poor.

Stanza 180 *Note* 61   St Dominic here symbolizes the Inquisition and makes this stanza heavily sarcastic.

Stanza 184 *Note* 62   Alain Chartier, the poet, left for lovers in his *La Belle Dame sans Merci* the making of songs and ballades.

Stanza 186 *Note* 63   For this play on ducks and geese, compare *Le Lais*, stanza 16. It is interesting also to compare it with 'Galen might go shooe the Gander for any good he could doe' from 'The Unfortunate Traveller' by Thomas Nashe. Or more recently: 'Love likes a gander and adores a goose' from Theodore Roethke's 'I knew a Woman' (see also *Le Testament*, stanza 167).

Stanza 203 Note 64 These remarks on illness have led to the conjecture that Villon suffered from syphilis. Though highly probable, it cannot be ascertained. Some readers take *Ballade: To his Girl-friend*, stanza 100, as equally suggestive.

Stanza 205 Note 65 Red was the colour in which martyrs were mourned. It is a joke here for the martyr to love (see *Le Lais*, stanza 6). According to some medieval falconers, a merlin was the ideal bird for a lady! The envoy gains point if this is accepted.

EPISTRE

1 This epistle was most likely written during his imprisonment at Meung in the summer of 1461. Even here, Villon cannot resist taking several knocks at his friends.

QUATRAIN

2 This was composed in his imprisonment in the Châtelet towards the end of 1462. He had been arrested for a minor brawling incident with a papal scribe Ferrebouc who, unluckily, had influence. He was tortured and sentenced to be strangled and hanged. The second line makes Paris a village in the district of Pontoise, but, more seriously, hints that things would have been differently handled in Pontoise which comes under the king's direct jurisdiction, unlike Paris.

L'EPITAPHE

3 This was written during the same imprisonment.

Notes

LOUENGE A LA COURT DE PARLEMENT

4 I have translated this in a more ironic style than is normally done because I cannot believe Villon is serious. The reference to his teeth implying 'chokepear' treatment supports me. 'Ange' is also slang for law enforcement officers. It is worth comparing line 2 with stanza 38 of *Le Lais*.

QUESTION AU CLERC DU GUICHET

5 Villon appealed against the sentence of death and parliament set the judgment aside. This ballade is addressed on his release to the gatekeeper of the Châtelet, a man not without previous convictions. Villon's sentence was commuted to banishment for ten years from Paris.